To

Th                  for being
a  beta-reader for this little
tale!

*Rixi*

# Perception Prism

## A Novella

# Rixi Hazelwood

Perception Prism by Rixi Hazelwood

Copyright © 2023 Rixi Hazelwood

All rights reserved. No portion of this book, or the original posting on the online self-publishing platform Royal Road, may be reproduced in any form without permission from the author, except as permitted by UK copyright law.

Cover by Eliushi from @eliushi.draws

Also by the author:

Novellas
*Lanterns of the Lost*

Novels
*Dreamsmiths*

All works are available to read free online via Royal Road as well as being available to purchase on Amazon

*For anyone who has ever struggled to see their own beauty and worth. You are enough exactly the way you are.*

*For James, who inspired this story by seeing things in me I could only dream of believing but wished I could see.*

# ONE
## Alastair

*Is she OK?* Each step up the stairs is another beat of the same question. It's an eternal query, one Alastair is forever asking or biting back. Asking too often wears her down. It wears him down too, because the answer is invariably one he doesn't want to hear. They take things day by day, and there's a deep-seated ache for the answer to that question to be 'yes'. It plagues his daydreams, a wish so strong it sometimes brings tears to his eyes to imagine it. Two stairs left. *Get yourself together, Alastair. She needs you to be upbeat.* The door stands between him and the room she's been in for three days. What will he find this time?

The door pushes against the stale air, cutting through the blanket of defeat that fills their bedroom.

'Nik?' She's on her side, facing him, eyes glassed over in the dim evening of the room. She isn't there, at least not yet. He waits the customary few seconds or so for her to rouse from her stupor. Light and recognition creep into her eyes, and a weak smile that pains his heart works against the weight of her facial muscles. She pushes a hand across the bed towards him, reaching. 'How are you feeling?' A small shake of her head, but he catches it.

At this point, he's an expert at reading even her smallest expression. She snuggles up to him as he plants himself gently on the bed beside her. She used to feel warmer, in both temperature and personality. It's not forever. She's strong enough to fight it, but sometimes people need a break from fighting. This week is one of those weeks. He has to be here during those times, there are no half measures. He isn't a fair-weather partner.

The black screen yawns at them from its mounted position on the wall. No TV today, she can't even handle that much. She fiddles with the button on his blazer, idly running her finger around its edge. Repeated movements help her out of her daze, structure her mind. He holds her close and waits for her to come back to herself.

'How was work today?' She cuddles in closer, muffling the last word of the question.

'It was nothing too different, they were finalising some of the details for the trip.' *Why did I mention the trip? Mistake number one, you fool.*

'Oh...'

'I can tell them I can't go if you'd prefer me to stay home? I mean if you're still not feeling well.'

'No, don't be silly. I'll be alright, this is nothing. Give me a day or two and I'll be OK. I don't want to get in the way of your work.'

'You could never get in the way of anything.' Her ruffled hair tickles his lips as he kisses her forehead, and her face spreads into another weak smile. 'Have you eaten today?'

'Oh, no I don't think I have. I didn't realise what time it was until you got back.'

'Well, we have to fix that.'

'No I should make dinner, you've been working all day.'

'Shhh, no arguments, I'll be back in a little while.' He slides away from her, stroking her hair as she settles back on to the pillow. The coat-hangers rattle as he hangs his blazer back in the wardrobe. It's a tracksuit and t-shirt kind of evening, that's for sure. 'Alright, do you mind me opening the curtains?'

'No, I don't mind.'

'Let's get a little air in here, then I'll go and make us some food. Want me to switch on the TV?' Her head shakes "no" on the pillowcase. The dry air drains out of the window like water from a bathtub. 'That's better.' He leans over to kiss her cheek. 'I'll be back in half an hour.'

He holds the sigh in until he's downstairs, well out of earshot in the kitchen at the back of the house, whereas their bedroom is at the front. It pours out of him, leaving him deflated and tired. He really doesn't want to cook tonight, it's a job they usually share, but there's still no change. If anything she's worse today. No TV, no food, and no concept of passing time. He's seen her like this before… he's seen her worse than this before… when is it going to get easier?

Nikkita is so beautiful, the most beautiful woman he's ever seen both inside and out. Straight from the off he wanted to get to know her better. There's such a vibrancy about her, a kindness and a lightness that he can't forget. It made days like these, when he wouldn't recognise her if he didn't know her already, even harder. Cooking is only a minor distraction. Thoughts queue up in a traffic jam in his head, one after another, but none of them move anywhere. He stirs the pasta even though it doesn't need it, turns the chicken far too many times, and narrowly avoids screwing up the vegetables of all things.

Any solace to be found in the fact he's cooking for her is lost when he plates up. His portion is quite generous, one you'd expect for a man of six foot tall who values exercise enough to keep slim. Nikkita's is no bigger than what a child would eat, but to put any more in front of her will only be a waste. Over-facing her isn't something he wants to do, if she can manage what he gives her she'll feel better. She'll eat it just to see him smile even if she doesn't want it. It'll make him happy, to know she's finally eaten, but it'll be a hollow victory knowing it hasn't made a difference when it comes down to it. Or maybe it will, it's impossible to tell what she feels because she doesn't even know herself. It's all buried under the mask of the condition. It's crushing her.

*I'll dig her out as many times as it takes.*

He gathers the plates, cutlery and anything else they might need and treks back upstairs in a precarious balancing act. They have a dining room table, but they don't always use it. On days like today he doesn't even entertain the idea that Nik will come downstairs to eat.

'Smells good.' The tray of food wobbles in his grip. She's sitting propped up, has tidied her hair a little, and the TV is playing his favourite documentary-type show narrated by David Attenborough. A warmer, stronger smile welcomes him. He beams at her and it brightens her eyes. She's made such an effort in the half hour he's been downstairs. She's so strong. 'What did you make?'

'Chicken with a bit of pasta and veg.'

'Sounds like heaven. Oh, you brought yours up too? You don't have to, I know you don't like eating in bed...'

'Nonsense, I have a dinner date with a beautiful woman and David Attenborough. I can't think of anywhere else I'd rather eat tonight.'

They sit side by side, legs outstretched, plates either on their lap or resting on their chest. Nik smiles at the small portion.

'Thanks, it looks yummy.' As they watch the documentary together, every mouthful she takes increases Alastair's relief. At least she's eating something today. His eyes flick over to the pill packet on her nightstand. One less than yesterday. Good, she didn't forget.

There isn't much he can do when he's at work all day, but when he comes home there's plenty. Whether it's eating in bed or just being there to give her a simple hug. They chat between forkfuls of pasta.

'So they're finalising the trip at work?'

'Yeah, they want me and one other person to go, though they're making me decide who to take. I wish someone had just been assigned, it's getting a bit competitive.'

'I'm not surprised, this will be a big merger for the company. Who wouldn't want to go with the CEO to help secure it? They probably think it will get them moved up in the world, get them some cred.'

'"Some cred"... are you going gangster on me now?' Her laugh is salve to his worry.

'Oh yeah, definitely. Did they decide how long the trip

will have to be? They guessed a month or two, right? For all the negotiations?' The pasta on her plate becomes the most interesting thing in the world.

'Something like that. I'll tell you as soon as I know and we can talk about it, OK?' Her nod is automatic, but she doesn't look as disheartened as when he first broached the subject. He told her as early as he possibly could. The more time she had to adjust the sooner she could work on getting her worry under control. She didn't show it at the time. She's good at hiding stuff that worries her, especially if she thinks she should be supportive of it. It's to avoid making him feel guilty about the company doing well and him needing to take the trip in the first place. Her own feelings don't matter to her, it's like she puts herself last constantly. Her mood is sinking, pulling them both deeper into the mattress with its gravity. 'Don't worry, I'll be back well before our special day.'

'You will?' Her whole spirit lifts.

'I wouldn't miss our anniversary, not ever. I can't wait to celebrate nine years since the day you agreed to be my partner. We'll do something special, OK? Whatever you want.'

'It can't all be about me, it should be about both of us. We'll choose together.' Her plate is empty, her smile grows stronger still. Maybe tomorrow she'll start to feel better. She's had longer spells, and shorter ones.

'Alright, agreed.' She nestles into the crook of his arm once he clears the dishes to the bedside table.

'I should get back into the office tomorrow, you made it into such a beautiful room for me. I feel bad on the days

I don't work.'

'You can go back to work when you're ready. You weren't able to do any today?'

'I... tried to get up but...'

'It's OK. Do you have any deadlines coming up?'

'Hmmm, nothing pressing. I've never missed a deadline yet, but if I don't want that to change I need to do some work tomorrow. Can you get me up before you go?'

'You always wake up before me anyway, but I'll give you an extra nudge if needed.'

'Thank you.' She puts both arms around him and squeezes him tight. 'I love you, Alastair. You've given me so much. Days like today I feel like I give you nothing back.'

'Hey, you give me plenty just by being who you are, OK?'

'... OK.'

'I love you too.' It isn't long before she drifts back to sleep. Today won't be the day she gets out of bed. Now she's eaten she'll sleep until morning, but at least her intent to work tomorrow is there. That's something. A sign that she's trying to fight her way out of it, gaining a little ground towards feeling well again. He lies her down on the pillow, peeling himself away and hoping the dishes won't clatter when he moves them. He'll join her in bed in a few hours.

The dishes sit in the sink and the water flows over them even after rinsing them clean. Nikkita made a little headway today, but it's still winning out. Plenty of people hate illnesses, hate seeing what they do to those closest to them. Alastair is no different. If he could cure her, he'd do it without hesitation. There's no way to know if he's even helping her, or just hindering her recovery. The thing that stops the woman he loves from seeing how beautiful she is, what an amazing person she is, from seeing any value in herself at all. If he could give her one thing to fight it, it would be the way she looks to him. If he could rinse her mind clean of depression the way the grime was rinsed from the plates, he'd feel like the king of their little world.

# TWO
## Nikkita

*It's easy Nikkita... all you have to do is throw the covers back and stand up. That's all. Then you'll have done it, you'll have gotten out of bed. Won't that feel good? To actually do something? Stop staring at the gap in the curtains and get out of bed. One leg at a time.*

It takes a few more minutes of building up some kind of mental strength before one foot, then the second, meets with the softness of the carpet. Another few minutes of staring, here in limbo between where she's been for the past few days and where she could be today. The weight of the decision presses against her. A surge of determination stirs as she turns to look at her sleeping partner, a sliver of sunlight illuminating his bare back. If she can't do it for herself, she can do it for him.

*Get. Up. And. Do. Something.*

Disorientation from being horizontal for so long swarms her as she closes the gap in the curtains. She's up and a flicker of pride sparks, the uselessness draining away a little. A big victory to her, though probably not to others.

With barely a sound she gathers her slippers and a cardigan and creeps out of the room, padding softly down the stairs. At first, all there is to do is wander around the house like a stranger. There's a sense of having been gone for a long time. Alastair has kept things so clean. Little needles poke at her stomach. *He has so much work to do already at the office, and I let him come home and tidy up? I should make breakfast for him, he won't be up for another hour.* From room to room she wanders until she finds herself back upstairs standing in her home office. *I said I'd do some work today, I have a lot to do. No pressing deadlines though.*

The desk chair feels like someone else's it's been that long since she sat in it. The thin, incomplete layer of light dust on her diary is easy enough to wipe away. Flipping through the pages makes her heart flutter, she can't afford those three days she's just let crawl by. Or was it five? A week? She's not sure. There's nothing to be done to change it now, but it dampens her resolve. *So useless. Today I'd better get something done or I'll lose my clients. I've never missed a deadline and I'm not about to start now.*

Nikkita loves her work, and is grateful to be able to work for herself. Alastair has been more than happy to support her transition from employment to freelance. People pay a hefty price to have their audio files transcribed, and sitting and typing what you hear is one of the most relaxing jobs to have. At least, Nikkita thinks so.

All sorts of files have crossed through her hands and ears, from university lectures to interviews to people dictating fiction. More than anything else she likes going back to re-listen and confirming she got nearly everything right. Listening to the thoughts of others helps to block out her own. Getting a peek into their lives and helping them record it "on paper". Motivation pulses in the dusty cavern of her chest. She can fight it today.

Down in the kitchen the smell of bacon and eggs wafts around her. A sense of purpose quietly fuels her actions. Al will be awake soon, and breakfast will be ready when he comes down even if it's the only thing she manages today.

*OK, when Al's gone to work I'll make some toast, have a shower, and then sit down and do at least two hours of work. No excuses!* Just as the kettle's bubbling stops and the catch clicks, Alastair peers into the kitchen with a concerned look which melts into relief.

'You're up.'

'Morning.' She beams at him. 'Breakfast is almost done, bacon and egg sandwich. I hope that's OK?' He finishes buttoning his shirt and moves over to her, turning her away from the hob and embracing her with a happy tenderness.

'Of course it's OK. Best start to my day, coming downstairs and seeing you and smelling that delicious smell.'

She wraps her arms around his trim waist. *Why would seeing me make anyone's day better?* 'Kettle's boiled, I was going to make some coffee too.'

'You're spoiling me.'

*If I did it more often like a good partner should, he wouldn't think I was spoiling him.* 'You deserve it, you have a busy day today.'

'Yeah, they should be finalising the details, and telling me what day I have to go and how long I'll be there for. I'm sure it won't be for more than a month, two at the most.'

*Don't you dare change your facial expression. You can cry when he's gone.* 'Oh that's not so bad. I'll... miss you though.' *Don't leave me alone for that long.*

'I'll miss you too. I wish I didn't have to go.'

*So do I.* 'It's a great opportunity for the company if you can make the acquisition, right? Now get yourself away from the hob or your bacon will burn.' She elbows him playfully, wanting him to believe she's feeling better. It isn't a lie, she is feeling better than yesterday. Determination burns on a wick that's difficult to light, and even more difficult to keep lit.

As Alastair sits munching on the sandwich she made, the question rises. She feels it looming. It bubbles behind his lips until it spills out.

'How do you really feel about the trip, Nik?'

*He sees through me so easily.* 'I'll... find it hard, but wouldn't anyone? It's just a month or two, not really that long in the grand scheme of things. I'm sure I'll be alright.'

He considers her, his truth barometer pointing right at her. 'I'll make sure I'm back as soon as it's feasible. You feeling better today?'

'A little, but I'll take a little over not at all.' *He wants a different answer. He always wants the answer I can't give him, or at least haven't given him for a good while. I so want to be able to say it… but only when I mean it.*

'You did great to get up today, you know? You're strong.'

*For doing what millions of people do every day? Bet it doesn't take them so long to decide to get up.* 'I can't stay in bed forever.'

His eyes trace her as she inspects the marble patterning of the island countertop. She can't stop her eyes from glassing over. It's creeping back in again, fuelled by all the negative thoughts that toll like sour bells with each nice thing Alastair says. *Don't listen to them. Don't listen.* Even through the vulnerable exposure of the fact that he can tell when she hasn't said what she's truly feeling, she appreciates his persistence. He's always so busy with work, but never too busy to take a moment to let her know he can see that something's bothering her. She's never had to experience the hollow echo of neglect.

'For while I'm away...' he treads carefully, 'why don't you make a few plans with friends? Book some things in on the weekends so you have something to keep you busy. I'd hate to think of you just sitting and working and not having any company.'

*What friends? I haven't seen any of them recently.* 'Umm... yeah I could make some plans. I haven't seen the girls for a while.' *Not since I started getting ill more often.*

'They could make more of an effort. I've noticed they just come and go as they please.'

'Not Ellie, but she's in her busy season right now. As for the others... I guess it's hard for them when I'm...' *so depressing to talk to that they can't stand to be near me.*

'It's hard for you. You're the one trying to deal with it, and if they really are your friends they should be supporting you not turning tail when you're not well.'

'It's alright, I have you. I don't need anything else to help me get better.'

He smiles, brushing the crumbs off his hands and

straightening his tie. 'Thank you for breakfast. I love you, and I'll see you tonight OK?'

'OK. Love you. Have a good day at work.' As soon as he closes the door behind him and the lock clicks, the expanse of the house opens out around her. An echo chamber of space that she'll never be enough to fill by herself. She's back at the kitchen island, staring again at the pattern of the countertop.

*Remember what you said you'd do today. Don't let it stop you from doing those things. Just take it slow, one thing at a time. First was... toast. That's easy enough in theory.* The toaster springing makes her jump, and each crispy bite is punctuated with thoughts she can't control. *You're going to be alone for months...* crunch... *you'll only have yourself for company...* crunch... *no-one would want you for company...* crunch... *your company isn't worth anything...* crunch... *he'll enjoy having a break from you...* crunch... *from having to look after you as though you're a child.* The last slice of toast ends up in the bin in defiance alongside a muttered 'shut up!'.

A shower is next on the list. Why do all these things give her so much time to think? The hot water blasting down on her head and back is loud enough to drown out her thoughts. A simple but welcome pleasure. If only her mind could be cleansed the same as her body. A warm rush of water to pull out all the badness. She imagines it draining away, running off of her flesh and down the plughole in a swirl of dark, sad colours. How it would feel to be free, for Alastair to come home and see genuine happiness on her face. The happiness that's in her heart somewhere, buried, deep underneath the host that can't feel it. She'll beat it one day, in some dream or another. If she were stronger, maybe? Alastair said she's strong this morning, but that doesn't make it true.

The shower is refreshing and a little uplifting. The short break from the onslaught of negative commentary does wonders. Just one more thing on the list for today. Two hours of work, that isn't too much. Doing two today will mean she'll be capable of three hours tomorrow. *I'll do it, I'll get back to it and get those projects finished by the end of the week.* The steam from the shower warms the towel slightly, and as she wraps herself in it and moves to the bedroom a determined smile slips on to her lips. That's her first mistake.

The first thing she sees as she enters the bedroom is the full-length mirror on the inside of the wardrobe door that Alastair left open. Rooted to the spot she stares at her towel-clad form. The thoughts driven away by the shower broil in amusement.

*Disgusting. Look at yourself. Fucking ugly, overweight mess. Is this what you think Alastair deserves for a partner? Such a state. Drop the towel, go on, drop it and grimace at yourself. Turn sideways and see how fat you are, the only shape your body has is an unkempt one. How can you even stand to keep looking?*

Towel discarded and tears in her eyes, Nikkita scrambles for her pyjamas. She has to cover up, no one can see, not even herself.

The wardrobe door closes harder than intended. He wouldn't have done it on purpose. He knows how she feels about the full-length mirror. He can say she's beautiful all he wants but how can that be true? He can reason that she's a perfectly good size for her height, and from a fitness point of view she doesn't need to lose any weight at all. But can't he see it?

*How can he not see how ugly I am?* The tiny flame of determination that she's worked so hard to kindle is long snuffed out, its pathetic wick trampled under her hideous reflection. She still has to try, but she sits at her desk and a fog of nothingness wraps around her chest. The only thing her body can do is burst into tears and carry her on defeated legs back to the empty solace and failure of the bed.

# THREE
## *Alastair*

The office is busy. Buzzing with the upcoming excitement of the acquisition. Eager eyes follow Alastair, all wondering if they'll be chosen to accompany him on this new chapter in the company's success. He should be excited... he is excited... somewhere underneath his worry for Nik. She supports him, he's in no doubt about that. She always tells him as much. He's done well, supposedly, building up his company to this point in just ten years. The merger he'll be travelling to negotiate will make the company an international one. A huge step. Nik has been so thrilled about it and tries hard to hide her dread of living alone. He's considered sending someone else on his behalf... but that wouldn't be right. As the owner he should decide the future of his own company and be part of its making in person. That, and the fact that some deep part of him he seldom connects with wants to go. Wants the space.

'Alastair!'

A smarmy voice blares into his private office and Alastair resists the urge to cringe. Couldn't he at least call him "Mr Deene" like everyone else?

'Yes?'

'Can I get you a coffee this morning? The usual is it?'

'No thank you, Robert. I appreciate the offer, though.'

'Well if you're sure, just let me know if you change your mind.' The man winks and lingers a touch too long before striding away looking pleased with himself. Robert's a good worker, but ever the first to jump on an opportunity to brown-nose. It's easier to refuse anything he offers, and get it himself later on. Not to mention Alastair can't stand his over-personal demeanour. All the clapping on the shoulder and leaning in far too close during conversations and meetings. He rarely dislikes people, but Robert's efforts to advance through favouritism are so obvious even a child could spot them. Hard work would catch attention, not pandering.

'Morning, Mr Deene.' Alastair's assistant bustles in like a breath of fresh air, instantly diffusing the slimy feeling left by Robert's offer of coffee.

'Morning Derek, how are we looking today?'

Derek flips open a large A4 scheduling book and barely glances at it as he answers the question. 'It's a busy day. We need to organise the briefing packages for the managerial staff for while you're gone. We've had the final details in for the trip and you have two meetings tomorrow to go over the offer and negotiation plans with the rest of the board. Some of them are pushing pretty hard to add new elements to the deal.'

'Why am I not surprised,' Alastair groans, 'I bet it's Brunel?'

'Yep, same old story.'

'Did you say the details of the trip were finalised?'

'Yep, they booked you in to quite the swanky hotel, but that doesn't surprise me given that the other company have asked that you stay for three months.'

'Three months! Why so long?' A cold sweat rises on Alastair's skin.

'Apparently they want to take things slower since it will be such a big decision for them. They've scheduled you in for meetings with all sorts of different groups to do with the company, and also want a full run down of how you conduct your business and to hear all about your work ethic, yadda yadda the list goes on. They're being very cautious all of a sudden.'

'Thanks Derek, I'll contact them later and try and put their minds at rest a bit. Three months though… that's a long time to be away for a business merger. It's almost excessive.'

'Maybe you'll go in there and wow them so much you won't have to stay out there that long?' They share a chuckle.

'Well, that would be ideal, but if they're suddenly erring on the side of caution I imagine I have quite the amount of convincing to do. Companies sometimes panic near the end of acquisition deals, they feel they're losing themselves. They're probably just a bit spooked.'

Derek nods and excuses himself. He's the most efficient personal assistant Alastair has ever had. Maybe he should just take him on the merger trip with him? It was certainly a thought. He turns his gaze out of the window towards the rest of the business park. The city looms just beyond its bounds.

*Three months. Nik's already unwell. Can she handle being alone for that long? She seems better this morning, but a lot of it was façade. She thinks I'll be mad if she asks me not to go. I know I have to go it's just... ugh.*

He'll think himself in circles if he carries on. He does that often enough. The slowly filling inbox and proposals to read, budget reports, merger details... all the letters turn to sand and scuttle off the screens and pages. He has to clear his head first. Gathering his things he catches a confused look from Derek, who swiftly returns to his door with a questioning expression on his face.

'I'm heading out for the day. I'll brief the staff tomorrow between the meetings.'

A mild look of panic crosses Derek's face. 'Is everything alright? There's a lot on your schedule for today. Tomorrow will be a nightmare if you don't take care of some of it. Plus they're all waiting on bated breath to find out who you're taking on the acquisition trip. They've been staring at me since I got here as though I can tell them something they don't already know.'

'You can now, and get used to more staring. I'll take you with me, if you'd want to come?' The decision pleases Alastair as soon as the words leave his mouth.

'Me? But I'm not even a businessman, just a personal assistant.'

'Don't let me hear you put "just" in front of your job title again. You're such a huge help and have so much potential, Derek. You don't have to come, of course, but if I have to choose it's you I'm choosing. I'll try and come back this afternoon, I trust you to keep everything in line until then. Sorry to dump this on you, I just need to clear my head a bit. Tell anyone who asks that I've gone out, and if they insist on being given a reason tell them I had urgent personal business. Is that OK?'

'Y-yes. I'd love to accompany you on the trip, thank you Mr Deene. I'll make sure you're not disturbed today.'

Alastair pats Derek on the arm in gratitude as he leaves. 'I appreciate it. I'll be back later, or tomorrow, and then I'll get working on that to-do list.'

As the chatter of the office fades away behind him a weight lifts from his tired shoulders. He loves his job, his company, but he loves Nikkita more. Yet… there's a spark in him again that he isn't quick enough to stifle. A spark of relief and peace, anticipation even, at the thought of spending three months outside of the shroud of her depression. It's fleeting and small like a pin prick, but it's enough for him to feel the immediate sting of guilt and the rolling of alarm in his gut.

He can't shake her from his thoughts today. It isn't much, but he wants to find a gift. Something to apologise for having to go away. For thinking that tiny, horrible thought. Something that might make her feel good about herself for a change. She does sometimes, in brief spells, seem more confident but he still sees his compliments bounce off her like a squash ball off a court wall. Is there such a gift in existence that can get through to her? That won't make her feel guilty for receiving it? Enough with the imaginings, he'll just have to settle for a gift she'll really like. A new notebook? She's a bit of a stationery fiend. Perhaps one of those beautiful hardback ones he always forgets the name of. A new book? If only he'd checked how far she was through her current series, then he could make sure to get her the right one.

He meanders through the city, shop after shop passing him by, his head running a commentary on why they wouldn't sell anything good enough as a gift for Nik. It has to be something special, something to help her keep busy while he's away. Flowers will barely last a week, and certainly won't keep her busy. Maybe she could be encouraged to keep a journal? He circles back to the idea of a notebook.

The streets are packed with people. For a Tuesday morning that surprises him, shouldn't most people be at work? It's just a sign of how things are nowadays. The more pressing consideration for now is where the specialist stationery store is. He's been in there once with Nik, but didn't pay attention to how she led him there. Lost in his thoughts he wanders through the main shopping centre, equally busy as the streets outside it. How people can suggest the High Street is dying when there are this many people out shopping on a weekday is beyond him.

His puzzlement continues. Still no stationery store. As he weaves back onto the throng of the main outdoor walk a sigh escapes him. *I just wanted to do something nice for her and I can't even find the damn shop.* Perhaps there would be something handmade near the craft market instead. It's a little walk away, but he doesn't mind in the slightest. Head down, one step after another, and a barrage of bees in a hive of thoughts make the crowds seem quiet. It's only after several minutes that the sounds of the crowd vanish altogether, and he doesn't recognise the brick pattern on the ground. Or does he? It can't be this place.

Looking up confirms it, and the world jars around him. He can't be here, this is an entirely different part of the city, about three miles away from the main strip. His chest writhes. *OK, OK, just think about it. Could you have been walking for longer than a few minutes?* The time on his phone suggests not. There wouldn't have been time to walk all this way. *Think back, think carefully. Did you just get lost in worry?* Looking left and right he can't match the events in his head. He hasn't been walking long, and even if he isn't right about it only being a few minutes, it still wasn't long enough for him to end up here.

It's an old commercial street where all the shops have long gone out of business. A mosaic of boarded windows and spray-painted shutters. He has to move. Being in a place like this in a suit like his will get unwanted attention. He spent more time on this side of the city as a kid, and he hasn't forgotten the layout. His only choice is to start walking in the direction of the main city again.

The near-deserted streets rustle with unease, the prickle of paranoia tickles his neck. It's easy to get jumped around here. He checks every alley, every side street as he walks. Something catches his eye. What is that? A shop sign? There are businesses still operating even in run-down areas like this? The calming smell of incense wafts past him in a fragrant trail, the shop is actually open? He stops, transfixed by the idea of a pocket of commerce among the fallout of failed businesses. It's like seeing a lantern in the middle of a desert. The decision to make the journey into the tiny side street isn't his own. Maybe this little shop has something in it he can gift to Nik? Something you can't find in all the normal shops. As he gets close enough to read the sign it only seems more suitable. Trinkets of Truth. It's too intriguing to pass by.

The shop front is something from another time. Old wood-framed windows divided into small squares that aren't all quite the same size. A banner, also on a wooden plaque, with golden letters and ornate corner work. The incense is prominent but not imposing, and past the window display there's nothing but shelves stacked with strange and unusual ornaments. The display itself is baffling. The items are mainly small: trinkets, jewellery, many things he can't describe. Despite their strangeness, they're beautiful. Would Nik think so too? None of these items strikes him as being of any practical use, but he could get her both a trinket and a journal. A gift she could use and one she could treasure.

A tendril of caution roots him there, staring at the window display, pondering what the items are and where they came from. This shop wasn't here when he was a child, yet it looks as though it hasn't moved for centuries. Well set into the bricks, like something from Victorian London. Could it be some sort of scam? If it was he could just walk away, right? Leave the shop with a curt "thank you" and have done with. Make his way back to the city and stop trying to figure out how he crossed it in mere minutes. It could probably be put down to stress, worry, anxiety. Surely people lose pockets of their day all the time?

*I'll just take a quick look, and if it seems dodgy I'll leave.*

The pull of the shop, the air about it, is stronger than the warning thread of caution. He has to go in. There's no reasonable explanation as to why, but he has to. He isn't a man of fate, or believing in divine guidance, but there's no other reason why he ended up in this exact spot other than he was meant to. He can't pull back. Intrigue has him in its grasp and it has a strong grip. It appears to be a gift shop, and he needs a gift.

The dainty bell hanging from a swirl of rolled steel jingles in merriment as he pushes the sturdy wooden door open.

# FOUR
## Alastair

As soon as the door clicks closed the strange sensation that he's stepped into an isolated pocket of the world rolls over him. The flickering thought that he won't be able to exit the shop again thrives on the new quiet. *Don't be daft, Alastair, it's just a weird old gift shop. Probably run by some old lady with nothing better to do. Just look around quickly and then go.* Why should he be spooked? Gazing around the shop the answer is forgotten, and replaced by a rising tide of wonder and curiosity. The shelves and cabinets are mismatched, no two the same, like the items that sit upon them. It's only silent for a few seconds, and then a deep chittering begins. Begins, or resumes? Low resonant hums, tiny ticks, fervent clicking, baseline buzzing. Are the items... communicating? Come on Alastair, get real.

There are no items he can compare to anything he recognises, and those he does only remind him of other things in an abstract way. The first shelf he passes is adorned with jewellery boxes, strewn with patterns so intricate they could be a language. Compact mirrors, bendy pendants, and ornate trinkets he can't recall the shape of after looking away.

A muffled rustling from the rooms beyond the shop startles him as he reaches for a ring that looks as though it was carved from the mountains and immediately bound to a silver band. It could be the wild maze of reflections zigging and zagging off of the glass shelving, but he's sure its colour is changing periodically. Is someone coming back to the front of the shop? The movements quieten. It isn't a large room, but he's dwarfed by the menagerie of unfamiliar objects around him.

Still listening, one ear cocked towards the back room, a small object on a shelf further into the collection catches his attention. Its surface swirls with different shades of blue, and the more he focuses in on it the more it whispers to him. "I can help her, I can help her. Nikkita needs me". Which is ridiculous, but those subconscious intentions that dragged him into the shop are at work again. He mutters quietly to the object with each new step. 'Can you? Can you help her? Tell me how?' It draws him to it.

A presence trickles into existence behind the counter, one that makes him very aware of how close he is to the little object and how much he wants to take it. It's a woman, and she isn't at all old. Her beauty takes him by surprise as does her youth. Her skin has a healthy, rich colour to it, and long brown hair curls and tumbles over her shoulders, held out of her face by a thin bandanna-like headscarf. Her expression tells him he shouldn't even be in the shop.

'Oh I... I'm sorry, are you still closed? I can go if you are, I thought you were open.'

Her surprise turns to a welcoming smile. 'No not at all, forgive me. I just wasn't aware you were here else I would have welcomed you. You're a little early.'

'Oh, there were no opening times on the door, sorry.'

'Not that kind of early.' She flashes him a knowing look, waving away his confusion. 'So it's the prism that catches your eye?' Such a unique voice, low and colourful, flecked with the tiny impressions of an accent he can't quite place.

'The prism?'

'It usually knows when it's needed. Tell me, do you have someone who needs help? Someone you wanted to find a gift for?'

'I... yeah.' *How did she know that?*

'Everyone who comes in here is looking for something like that, and this is the only place they'll find it. Relax a little, I don't bite.' As she steps around the counter he drops his shoulders, not realising how tense he is. 'Tell me of the person you want to help and I'll tell you which item will be most suitable for them, though the prism is rarely wrong.' She speaks about the items like they have personalities, sentience. This morning can't possibly get any stranger.

He shouldn't discuss Nik with this woman, he doesn't know her. Then again she doesn't know Nik, so can it really be that harmful? There's a confidence about her, one that makes him believe she can help him. He doesn't have to say much, just enough for her to get the idea of what troubles Nik.

'My partner she... struggles a lot with depression. It affects how she sees herself, it has for a long time. She hates the way she looks sometimes, and doesn't realise how beautiful she is, how kind. She's the most amazing person I know, but she just can't see it. I wish... I wish she'd believe me when I tell her that. It bounces off her, or she gets that denying look as if she thinks I'm lying. She doesn't do it on purpose, I know it's part of the condition. I can't do anything to help her. Not a thing. Sometimes I even wonder if it's me that's making her unhappy.' He didn't mean to say quite so much. A weighty clod starts to swell in his stomach. Has he made Nik look bad? Sound like a horrible person? 'Sorry I didn't mean...'

'It's alright. Many of the people who come here have similar stories, Alastair. It's hard. Harder than people know, to live with someone affected by such things. All sorts of men and women have sat before me and told me how useless they feel. You are not the first and will not be the last. I understand.'

Someone who understood at last. 'Do you think you have a suitable gift?'

'I do. The prism is the right choice. It will be able to help your partner to change her view of herself.'

'Really? How?' In his excitement he bumps the shelf behind him and scrambles to steady it. She picks the prism up. The swirling colours on its surface stop moving.

It isn't quite as long or wide as her palm, but it fills most of her hand. A 3D diamond in shape with four triangular panels above and below the middle ridge. She holds it between her thumb and middle finger, each covering the point on either end of the little object.

'It has many qualities, but its main function is to show the one who holds it how the person who gifts it sees them. They will see themselves through the eyes of another. Nikkita will see herself the way you see her.'

'That's perfect!' A fever of happiness grips him, this is just the thing he's been hoping for! Something to help her see the truth, to make her see how skewed her perception of herself is. 'I'd like to buy it.'

'There is more to know first. The Perception Prism has rules, and you and your partner would be foolish to ignore them.' There's no malice in her voice, only knowledge and warning. 'No one else must handle the prism before you gift it to your partner. Only your hand must touch it. Your partner can only view the prism for one cycle. It will show her the image within it for a set amount of time, and she must respect however long that may be. If she wishes to view it again, she must wait at least one hour. It does not do well to overindulge in such things.

'Most importantly, she should never look into the prism while she is overcome with negative feelings about herself. She must view it while either neutral or in good spirits. It is a sensitive object with many layers of complexity. It has helped many and shown much, but to those who break the rules it will show nothing and do no good. Do you understand?' To think such a tiny item has rules. He tries to remember what she said, and found a summary ringing clear in his head. *Only you must touch it, she can only view one cycle at a time, she should never view it when in negative spirits or when feeling hatred towards herself.*

'Yes... I understand.' She offers it to him, and it's warm in his hand. A low hum seeps from it and its weight increases just slightly. 'What's it doing?'

'Don't worry about it, there is much that would take

too long to explain.' After a few seconds she holds out a small gift box, signalling for him to place the prism inside. She seems reluctant to touch it again.

'Are all the items here like this? Where did they all come from?'

'I have worked long and hard to build up my collection, travelling all over the world. These items come from a different time, but their gifts are always needed. You know the rules, that's enough. Don't underestimate the prism, and don't stray from the rules, the rest will follow. I hope it manages to help your partner.'

'How much is it?'

'Your presence in my shop has been enough to pay for the item, but if you wish there is a box on the counter that patrons often choose to donate to instead. I have a delivery to attend to, thank you for your custom, Alastair.' The beautiful woman disappears again into the mysterious back rooms. There's no price on what she's supposedly given to him, and the donation he puts in the box is more than generous. With excitement in his chest and a few steps the tinkle of the bell announces his departure and the sweeping air of outdoors blusters around him. The fog of incense is blown away like cobwebs under a hearty duster, and as he exits the side street and walks away a pin of suspicion bursts his hopeful bubble.

*What just happened in there? No one just gives things away for free... was I ... tricked? Could it all be a scam?* The more he thinks back on it the more none of what the woman said made much sense. Was it the incense? Had it muddled his mind? She'd explained the rules of the prism and he'd lapped it up, believing every word. Could it really do what she said? It sounded impossible. He had to clear things up, make sure she wasn't praying on troubled people like himself, giving them false hope. The gift in his pocket seems a grand lie all of a sudden. A deceptive scheme. He plays it over and over in his mind as he walks but when he turns to go back to the shop, outraged that someone would pretend they could help Nikkita, he bumps into a woman laden with shopping bags.

'Oh, I'm so sorry.'

'It's alright, no harm done.' His stomach flips. He's back in the bustling hub of the city centre, standing in the middle of the commercial throng. Turning on the spot like a lost child he ambles towards the nearest bench and sits down, taking deliberately slow breaths. He's back on the main walk… three miles away from the little shop… again in a matter of moments. The paint of the well-worn bench flakes under his palms as he squeezes the lip of the seat… one more detail turns him cold. She referred to him by name, but he never introduced himself.

# FIVE
## *Nikkita*

*It's today. He's leaving today. Don't be clingy. You'll be OK. It's just three months, it won't be a problem. You can handle this.* Nikkita's mind races as Alastair runs through his final checks. He has all his travel documents, all his important papers for work. She makes sure to ask him if he has his laptop and all his chargers, plenty of stuff to entertain him on the flight. He says he'll probably sleep.

He's worried about her, it's plastered all over his face, trying so hard not to step on the explosive eggshells around her. She has to keep her brave face on a little longer. He'll feel better if he thinks she's feeling OK about it.

'OK, I think I've got everything.'

*Don't leave me here on my own.* 'Will you keep me updated? Let me know when you take off and land, and when you get to the hotel?'

'Of course.'

'I'm... going to miss you a lot.' *I can't handle three months alone.*

'I'll miss you too, Nik. So much.' He sweeps her into a tight embrace.

*Don't cry. Just hold up a bit longer.*

'I'll call you when I've settled in, if it's not too late for you here.'

Her throat clutches around her words. She follows him to the front door, helpless and full to the brim. When his suitcases are on the step he turns and holds her close.

'I love you, Nik. Remember what I told you last night?'

The little box sits in her dressing gown pocket and she wraps a hand around it with care. 'Yeah.'

'OK. I'll be back before you know it.'

They share a deep kiss. Cradling the gift box to her chest she fights tears as he packs himself into the waiting taxi. Her heart thunders as the car pulls away, she can't even raise a hand to return Alastair's wave. When the car is out of sight, taking her only company for the next three months with it, she steps back inside and hesitates. The door snaps closed like that of a cell. She sinks to the ground holding her stomach as it folds in a wave of loneliness. The house, in its new state of emptiness, throws every sob back at her from its silent corners. Alastair is no longer here to absorb them and make them go away. There's only her own company. She hates that. She hates herself.

As the dread builds, her mind furnishes her with the memory of the night before. Dishes wiped clean of a wonderful meal cooked by Alastair sit on the coffee table, and a warm blanket envelopes them both. They snuggle together in the flickering lights of the film that Nik isn't paying the slightest bit of attention to. There's an elephant in the room, shuffling awkwardly in the corner trying to hide in the shadow of a lamp. Alastair refuses to ignore it.

'Nik?'

'Hmm?'

'I have something for you.'

'Oh?' They sit up together, still draped in the warmth of the blanket. Alastair opens a drawer under the coffee table and produces a small box, placing it in her palm.

'I know you'll find it hard while I'm gone, no matter how much you tell me you're fine. I wanted to get something for you, but nothing seemed good enough. Then I found this strange little shop and this seemed perfect, but... I don't want you to open it yet.'

'When can I open it?'

'Open it when I'm gone, and when you feel a bit better. Don't look at it when you feel really sad, and don't look at it more than once an hour, OK? It's important that you remember that.'

'W-what is it?'

'You'll see. At least I hope you will. It's something to remind you of what you mean to me, but if you open it too soon then it won't work. Remember, only when you feel a little happier. Promise me?'

'I promise... and thank you. I love you.' He pulls her close to him again and she's careful not to crush the box between them.

If only she could return to that moment again and stay there. The hallway floor has become comfortable in the amount of time she's sat with her back to the front door. Would it really be so bad to stay there? To not have to think about anything other than the slight draft reaching under the foot of the door, or the bristles of the mat that were probably giving her bottom the texture of orange peel through her pyjamas? That wouldn't be so bad at all.

She promised him, though, that she would try her best. That she'll "feel better" as though it was something that'll just happen if someone wishes it enough. He doesn't expect that. She doesn't deserve his understanding, but hopes that he knows how much easier he makes things for her. They've spoken in the past about what he can do to help. It isn't surprising that he felt useless in the face of her depression when it reared from the depths of her mind for the first time. It's such a rollercoaster for him. Months of her being the woman he fell in love with, and then he gets stuck with what she sometimes fears is her true self. Snappy, moody, utterly joyless and empty. Why does he even love her at all? What is she offering? Nothing. Nothing but the misery she can't even feel anymore.

*That's right, he can't love me. No one can. I'm unlovable, unbearable. How does he put up with looking at me? What kind of reward am I for his commitment?*

The tears renew, rolling down her face, unwiped, unwanted. A deep well opens up within her. She lies back, allowing herself to totter on its edge. Should she just let go? Give in? Stop fighting it?

It's so much more exhausting to fight it than to let it take her. The emptiness whose hollow embrace will pull her away from the world and cradle her until the storm has passed. *Enough!* She scrambles away from the well. *Not today. Not again. Alastair will be back in a few months, I need to be better before then. Keep the house clean, keep our home safe. Keep myself well. I have to do it for him. Do everything for him. Get up! Get up and go about your day. Make a cup of tea, that's step one.*

*If you can do that the rest will come.*

She turns the gift box idly in her shaky hands. Just what did he buy? The only way she can find out is by trying her best to lift herself back into normality. With leaden limbs she pushes herself on to all fours, crawling towards the banister and wiping her tears away. Standing, straining against the boulder on her back, she succeeds. Every movement echoes through the empty house. To fight the silence she has to keep busy.

The box moves with her from room to room, a little guardian motivating her to keep moving. One menial task after the next, rewarding herself with positive words after each one. It's something Alastair came up with to help her kick herself back into action.

"It's OK to reward yourself for even the smallest task, Nik. Anything you can do on the days you want to sit and do nothing. Whether it's just going downstairs to eat breakfast, having a shower, folding washing while you sit in bed. Anything to get you moving, to occupy your mind. Think of it like a kick-start."

He started researching how to help a partner with depression soon after the first time he saw her in its throes. It upset him to see such a change in her. He asked if he was the problem, and the question had made her cry so much he thought the answer was yes. They cried together, but when she calmed down she explained. Explained the guilt she had from making him feel that way, that she was sorry she didn't know why she was so sad but she couldn't find the reason. She only knew he wasn't the cause. He's her only salve. The only one who can get through it. The only one she doesn't entirely lose sight of in those times. He's her only reason to do anything some days.

The washing is folded, another load put in the washer. The meagre breakfast dishes are clean and laid on the drying rack. Even if it did take her half an hour. The darkness of the bedroom keeps calling, longing to draw her back into its clutches. Her solution is to go and open the curtains, the windows, and strip the bedding off. Now there's less chance of failing. When the chores are spent she counts her little victories. Five, if you count actually getting up from the hall floor. Some might say that was the biggest victory of all. It had certainly been the most effort. The more she does, the more she wants to do, the more she believes she can do.

Without over-thinking it she walks into the office and sits at her desk, consulting the Paperblanks diary and considering how much work she needs to do to get the items back to her clients on the original deadlines. Usually she returns them early, but this time she'll simply aim not to be late. Just two hours a day for the first project, and one hour a day for the other. That will keep her on track. Three hours a day, that's all she has to do.

*You can't do it.*

*I can.*

*Why do you think that? You've done nothing to prove that's true in over a week. A week wasted rotting in bed where you belong.*

The gift box is light, but somehow heavy at the same time. *I have Alastair here with me still, in this gift. His encouragement is here. I have something to aim for now. But... it only makes me miss him more.* The determination that had been snuffed out sparks once more. If she wants to know what's in the box, she has work to do.

# SIX
## Nikkita

Nikkita stretches in her office chair, finally finishing with one of the two projects looming in her diary. The last few days have been a whirl of productivity, and the heavy cloak around her has lifted. It's no more than a summer shawl now.

The house has been partially deep-cleaned, and with the few hours' work she put in this morning one more job is off her books. It just needs returning to the client. For the rest of the day relaxation is in order.

Alastair kept her up to date as promised. There were only minor delays to his flight, his hotel is swanky, a suite since he's staying so long, and he's grateful for it. *He sounded so tired when he called, hopefully he manages to rest up and adjust to the new time zone. It's important that he gets a break while he's there, at least between the negotiations. He deserves that much.*

*He deserves a break from you.*

It creeps in, an insidious commentator that waits, lurks behind every thought ready to pounce. 'He doesn't want a break from me. He misses me, he would have stayed here if he could. He's still with me, that's his choice. He chooses me every day that we're together.' Out-loud contradictions are another of Alastair's ideas. They help a lot. She might seem like she's arguing with no one at all, but stamping out those thoughts is satisfying. A genuine smile breaks the neutral expression her face has assumed for days, and her spirit soars just a little. A leap from one branch to another. 'Once I've sent this email... I'll open the gift.'

The sofa dips as she settles in to it with the gift box. She's feeling better, a thought that by itself makes her feel even more so. When she messages Alastair to thank him later, he'll also know as well and then they'll both be happy. The television drones on, some show she's seen several times. Suspense and excitement seep from the box. It isn't wrapped, but a tiny ribbon seals it. Pulling one taper and untangling the deep green decoration, her heart flutters. Lifting the lid seems forbidden after waiting so long to open it. The moment of truth.

Sitting in the box is a... well, she isn't sure what to call it apart from it being beautiful. An octahedron with eight triangular panels, each one with a gold trim around its edges. Four meet at a point at the top, and four at the bottom. She can hold it between her thumb and middle finger, turning it to look at the melding blues that change hue with every direction it's tilted in. Even when it's still the surface swirls, as though thinking and calculating. In the box a tiny card reads "The Perception Prism". It's a prism? Like something that reflects light? Surely it has to be more than that, as pretty as it is. Maybe she's missing something?

There are no buttons, or instructions. Even if it is just an ornament, it's a lovely gift. Maybe if she puts it in the sunlight it'll cast patterns on the walls. The more she inspects it, the more it hums in her hand. Holding it horizontally she takes each half between the fingers of both hands, looking for anything written on any of the panels. With as much care as she can she tries twisting it, it's large enough for something to be concealed inside. It's embarrassing to think that she might be staring in wonder at a box within a box. Small mechanical ticks register as she moves each half in opposite directions. It's opening!

After a quarter-turn the panels on one half of the prism spread open like a blooming flower. There's nothing inside it, but at least now she can stand it up and it will support itself. It sits awkwardly on her palm, but as it stands upright one panel from the top half opens. A little drawbridge being dropped, and colours corral together inside the curious item. A need to peer into it sweeps over her and she lifts it to her face, looking in with one cautious eye.

Within the prism is a woman. Stunning, vibrant and happy. It's a windy day and the breezes toy with her mid-length sandy-blonde hair. The sun douses her face, and warms the clothes that cover her slim body. She holds the hand of someone, a hand that Nik recognises. The watch is the same one she bought for Alastair on their third year together. The thought that echoes in the prism is his voice, too. "I love you, Nik". *This is... me? This is how Al sees me? I look nothing like this person, she's so... gorgeous and vibrant.* The light within the prism begins to fade, the image rippling and disappearing into the dark. As she moves it away from her teary eye the panels close and it's a diamond shape once more. Moving to turn it again, to bring the image back, she hesitates. The rules Alastair gave her patter across her mind. *Don't look at it more than once an hour.* Why? Why isn't she allowed to see it again for an hour? She has to see it again so she can be sure that woman isn't her.

Placing the prism back in its box gently she rushes to the mirror in the hall. The image from the prism is impossible to overlay with the reflection. Dank, unbrushed hair, pale skin, empty eyes and still carrying a few more pounds than she wants. It's like trying to match a tracing to an original when one of the images is upside down. Yet... there are flashes of herself in the woman from the prism, and the day from the scene is clear in her memory. They'd gone out for the day, exploring a beach on the coast, laughing at the force of the wind that was blowing in off of the sea.

The image turns the right way up, and falls on top of her own reflection. It really was her. When she recalls what she saw again and again something swells in her chest and spills out as soft tears. They travel down her smiling cheeks. From her mouth comes a phrase that she's never once uttered in her life. 'I actually looked pretty.'

*No you didn't, who are you kidding?*

'I did. I... do. In his eyes... I am beautiful.' The voice in her head has no retort. A drop of confidence falls into the pool of her self-perception. Her reflection changes even as she looks at it, just slightly. Her hair a bit brighter, eyes more alive. She can't wait for another hour to pass, but she will. Until then, she only has the memory of it.

# SEVEN
## Alastair

Quiet, solace... and relief. That's what the hotel room brought for Alastair at first. The very air seemed lighter now that it wasn't choked by Nik's depression, the ground blessedly free of eggshells, and for several days part of him had revelled in that. A layer of tension had carried itself away as he lay around watching TV or went to eat in the hotel restaurants with a feeling of peace about him. It didn't last long though.

Far from home, far from Nik, and stuck for another eleven weeks. A longing for her started creeping in. When he comes home at night he wants to see Nik, not a freshly made bed and new towels on the rails. Her hair always either a mess or totally neat. The smell of whatever she's cooking filling the house on the days she's out of bed, or going upstairs and seeing her frowning in concentration as she works at her desk. Even the days she retreats to the bed entirely, he still gets that little snuggle when he plops down next to her. Here he gets nothing. Emptiness, just like Nik has at home.

His watch tells him it's almost time to call her. They speak every few days, messaging in between, not wanting to rack up too much of a bill even if he's able to claim it back on expenses. Nik has been improving little by little each time they talk, and is more upbeat in their text conversations. That can change from day to day. Is she putting on a front? In person there's no question of when she's truly OK and when she's pretending. Over the phone it's harder. She doesn't do it to be deceptive, she does it to protect herself. To protect him. It both touches and annoys him at the same time. If she can't act the way she feels around him, then does she truly feel safe with him?

His mobile lights up a second or two before the buzzing begins. She's calling him, something must be wrong.

'Nik? Are you alright?'

'Yeah, I'm fine. You sound worried, what's up?'

Relief settles around him. 'It's nothing just, with you calling me I thought...'

'Everything's OK here. How was the meeting?'

'It was OK, but they seem to be getting more and more skittish as the negotiations start. What have you been up to?'

'I finished the work for the bigger transcription job and... I opened my gift. Thank you so much, Al. It's so beautiful.'

'You felt well enough to open it? Wait, you did work today?'

'I did. I managed to do some work three days in a row. Your gift has made me feel so much better that I might even be able to work for the rest of the week, too.'

Her voice is back to its vibrant tone, she sounds herself again. The prism had been the right choice, he'd actually done something to help her. He holds back the tears.

'That's amazing, Nik! You got the whole thing finished?'

'Yeah! I've been using all the little methods you taught me, if I'm any better at all it's because of you.'

'Hearing you sound so well has really made my day. I'm proud of you.'

'You are? What for?'

'Because you fought back and you kicked depression's arse this time, you're strong and stunning and amazing.'

'The image in the prism... it took me a while to believe it was me to be honest. I see it now, though, and I couldn't have seen it without you. You've been telling me for a long time that I'm not ugly. I guess I just had to see it to accept it.'

She won't accept it that easily, he knows that much. She sounds so happy that in the moment she may be finding herself prettier, but it won't be enough to change her entire view of herself. That's not how it works.

The high is more than welcome, but what'll happen when it wears off? When her negative perception starts doubting what she saw, starts fighting and telling her that it's all a lie.

He's seen it happen before, when he tells her she looks pretty as they prepare to go to weddings or parties, and through the night she'll come to doubt it more and more. Bit by bit. By the time they head home, sadness sinks back into her features and she goes straight upstairs to get rid of the clothes and make-up she feels are pointless adornments that do nothing to hide her ugliness.

'Just don't start doubting it. You deserve to know how

beautiful you are. It's late for you, want me to let you sleep?'

'I'll remember. I can't forget now I have your gift. I didn't realise the time, yeah I'll go to sleep. I want to get up a little earlier, start getting back into my old routine. Do you have a meeting tomorrow?'

'Not tomorrow, but in a day or two we have the first serious negotiation where they come back with their terms.'

'You'll do great. Speak to you on the weekend?'

'You bet. Night.'

'Night.'

As soon as the phone-line closes loneliness presses in on him again. Speaking to Nik had pushed it out, giving him a protective bubble. The lack of her rings out in the silence. The channels on the hotel TV are different than the ones they have back home. Flicking aimlessly through them he settles on a programme about a pair of guys who buy and restore old or vintage items. The slightly earlier finish from work is welcome. Sitting around a table discussing the terms his company have laid out to the acquisition they're approaching has drained him. Watching the reaction of each of the new company's board members, trying to read how they feel about it through their reactions and in between the lines of their responses. What will they come back with in two days' time?

Despite the loneliness encroaching around him, a big weight lifts from his exhausted shoulders. Nik seems so much better. The shop the prism came from frequents his dreams. Trying to make sense of it is pointless, but in a way he doesn't want to. How often can something perfect fall into the laps of those searching for it? It might not completely solve Nik's problems, in fact he highly doubts it will, but it's already helped and that takes some of the pressure off of him.

Living with someone with depression isn't something he ever expected to have to handle when he met Nik. She's the life of a room when she laughs, her smile triggers others to do the same, reaching out and cheering people up, drawing them to her. How is he the one to have the honour of being with her? The first time he saw her in a deep depression he felt so helpless. That helplessness never abates. The guilt never goes away. Guilt that he can't seem to make her happy, that he can't make her see her worth. That sometimes he's had enough.

The staccato buzz of the phone is a beacon in the monotony of the hotel. It's just a message, but Alastair almost jumps for his phone. It's been a while since he's seen that number, a year or two at least, but he's very glad of it. Edward is an old school friend. They met up every few years. He's currently working for a company in the same city. When had that happened? Last time they spoke he'd been planning to move somewhere entirely different. Though thinking about it he had mentioned the possibility of having to travel for work if he got the promotion he wanted. He was just checking in, mentioning that they should meet up soon when he returns home for a vacation. They can do better than that since this coincidence has fallen upon them. Just wait until he tells him he's in the same city and free to meet up any evening in the next few months. Sometimes the world is a small place. Catching up with Ed will be one distraction at least. It's been an age since he had a lad's night out.

# EIGHT
## Nikkita

'Are you listening, Nikkita?'

'Yes, sorry, I'm listening.'

'I was saying that this woman the other day gave me a look as though I was something mouldy she found in the fridge just because I happened to get the last silk scarf from Selfridge's. Honestly you'd think she was going to slap me then and there, but it's first come first serve. She stepped away to go and ask the price but you just don't ask the price of things in there, if you have to ask you aren't going to be able to afford it anyway. She would have been better off somewhere more on her level.

'Rick is being so unbearable lately too. He says work is busy and he's tired but he's barely giving me any attention and I just feel so unloved. He comes home and goes to bed really early after he's eaten and he never cooks dinner for me now. It's me every night without fail.'

Emma can whine for hours. Incessant, constant and petty. On and on and on. It's a struggle to keep calm. The more she drones the more the small pile of happiness Nik built seems to dwindle, but at the same time things cross her mind that normally wouldn't. Retaliation against Emma's never-ending issues threatens to pour out of her mouth in place of the sympathy she's forcing forward.

'Didn't you say he's coming up for a promotion and

that's why he's doing the extra hours?' Nik asks carefully.

'Yeah he is, he's been told the promotion is ready and waiting for him if they can close this deal.'

'I'm not surprised he's tired, then. I wouldn't want to cook after working overtime.'

'He should still make the effort to cook for me sometimes. Besides, you work from home, it's not like it's a problem for someone like you. Rick goes out to a real office every day, but that doesn't mean he should let home life slip.' *Someone like me... real office. She's obviously looking down her nose at me. Doesn't stop her drinking my coffee or inviting herself over, though.* 'His idea of cooking for me was bringing home a takeaway.' Emma tuts in disgust. Had Alastair worked late Nik would have no qualms at all about cooking for him when he got home.

'At least then neither of you have to cook, and you can sit and eat together.'

Emma scoffs, slipping a strand of her chocolate brown hair behind her ear. 'For all the good that does, he barely talks, just eats and goes to bed. Honestly, he's making no effort at the moment.'

'Sounds like his effort is all going into the promotion, which is understandable. He's just tired like you say. Probably stressed too. Once he gets the promotion I'm sure things will return to normal a bit more.'

'They'd better, I didn't get married to end up spending every evening alone or cooking late, slaving away all day only to have to continue it at night.' A puckered smear of dark red lipstick taints the rim of Emma's mug.

'How's your job going?'

'My job? Honestly Nik you clearly don't use Facebook enough. I quit my job last year and I'm a full-time housewife now. Honestly, I barely get a moment to myself. Between all the appointments and meetings with the other girls. I'm in the gym at eight in the morning and then it's home to clean the house and socials take up so much time.' Each time she says the word "honestly" Nik tries not to grimace. Yet she eyes Emma's trim, flawless figure with longing.

'Socials?'

'Wow you're out of all the loops aren't you? Instagram is where the people are at the moment, Nik. It's a full-time business keeping up appearances, I'm promoting my own little business on there. At least Rick doesn't have to worry about constantly keeping traffic moving through his social medias. I'm never free of notifications or having to vet who I follow or who follows me. It's a nightmare, so stressful honestly.'

*Don't roll your eyes, just don't. She really thinks that being a child-free housewife and a social media addict is harder than her husband's job? If she cleans her house every day it can't possibly take her more than an hour to get the housework done. She expects me to believe she isn't just coasting on his money?*

'So how do you fill your days? Sounds like things are busy?' Nik decides to push the issue, satisfying the itch of annoyance with her calm, innocent questions.

'Oh there's so much to do as a housewife, I can't even tell you.'

'But if you clean your house every day then it can't get that dirty?'

Emma laughs, taking care not to spill any coffee on her spotless, form-fitting dress. It seems more fitting to a business meeting than a house-call.

'Oh Nik, I don't clean, but I have to organise the cleaners to come in every other day and they need careful supervision. It's three hours on my feet instructing them as they go and then the time afterward making sure they've done everything right. Oh and honestly my mother is being a nightmare right now, every other day she needs something fetching from here or there. I feel like her personal summons.'

'How is your mother?'

'She's not well, but she's not exactly making the effort to improve either. You can't just let illness get the better of you.'

Emma has clearly never been truly unwell a day in her life. Nik doesn't like to make assumptions, but the way Emma references her mother's illness makes it sound like more than a mild ailment. Is there nothing in her life this woman is happy with? She isn't rich, but it's obvious that she lives very well indeed if they can afford for her not to work. Nik bobs one leg up and down. She's tiring of Emma's definition of a "problem". She appeared out of nowhere this morning after ten months without a single word, despite how much time she claims to spend on social media. It's true Nik hasn't made any effort to contact her either, but Emma is... hard to deal with and Nik hasn't been in the best place to deal with company for a while. Now that she's here on the sofa without so much as a hint of compassion, Nik begins to remember why that is. She has to get away from her even for a few moments.

'Would you like another coffee, Emma?'

She peers into the mug and purses her top lip, likely considering whether it can even be called coffee.

'Yes, I suppose I will, thank you. Where's Alastair today?'

'He's away on a business trip for a few months.'

'A few months! Is that man ever around to look after you and help out with things?'

'He's working very hard, and this merger will mean big things for his company. I happen to fully support him.' She snatches the cup away too sharply. Emma's eyebrows rise while she flounders with what to say. Nik doesn't give her the chance to respond, but strides into the kitchen and places the cup down next to the kettle, gripping the counter-top edge, gritting her teeth.

*How dare she suggest he doesn't look after me! How dare she assume anything about our life, about Alastair. She hasn't once asked how I am, how he is, anything about either of our lives. She just turns up and complains that her husband works too hard to cook and her mother is too ill to manage alone and goddamn strangers scowling at her for the sake of a silk scarf. She has no idea... no idea what it's like. Am I being a bitch here? Maybe she really is struggling with what's going on but I just can't see how any of the things she's mentioned are things to complain about. Am I just being narrow-minded? Self-absorbed?* The voice rose from the depths of its increasing silence, counter-thoughts seeping in to answer her questions.

*Yes. Yes you are. You always are. You never think of others, only yourself and your issues. There's no kindness in you.*

*There is! I want to listen and help her if I can but... she never contacts me apart from when she needs to vent about this ridiculous stuff. Otherwise I never hear from her at all. I might be empathetic and quiet, too scared to tell her I don't want to hear it today, but I know when I'm being used. This woman isn't a friend, she's just using me.*

*You aren't good for anything else. She's come to you for help and you're turning her away.*

*She's come to me to make herself feel better about her life. I've seen how she looks at our home, even the coffee isn't good enough for her. She doesn't think my job is real, she doesn't think Alastair is ever home. Why... why do I care what she thinks? Why do I keep calling her a friend? Maybe she's my only friend.* She searches her mind for other people to attach the label to. Very few come to mind. None that she's seen for a long time, many had flaked away after visiting while she wasn't well. *There's only Ellie, but she's so busy I don't like to bother her.*

Ellie checked in with her a few weeks ago after she found out Alastair was going away. She's travelling herself for work as a wedding planner and it's busy season, but she promised she'll contact Nik as soon as she's home again. Ellie always sticks to her word. At this moment Nik wants nothing more than to have Ellie here, someone who actually understands her and genuinely cares.

The kettle clicks, though she doesn't recall filling and

boiling it. The coffee is in the mug, the sugar melding with it. When did she do all that? She's spilled some of the granules, probably in her anger. *Collect yourself. Just go back in there and listen to her, be a little more supportive, and she'll leave when she's done. You won't see her again for another year most likely or until she needs something.* She slips some extra coffee in for the bitterness and takes a deep breath before heading back to the front room.

'What's this curious thing? It looks quite expensive.' The mug lurches in Nik's grip. She left the prism next to a photograph of her and Alastair. Now it's in Emma's hands.

'What are you doing?'

'I was just having a look around while I waited. What is it? Is it rare?'

'Put it down.'

'Look at the lovely golden trim. Honestly, I wouldn't expect you to own such a thing.'

'Put. It. Down. Please.'

'Maybe you have some taste after all.'

'Put it down!' The coffee is long forgotten, sitting in a pool of itself on the dining room table. Emma's brows crease at Nik's tone, which has a malicious edge.

'I'm simply admiring something you own for a change, why is it such a prob-'

A fire sparks to life in Nik's chest, and there's no desire to smother the flames. 'Get your hands off it and get out.'

'What?'

The beautiful image of Alastair's perception from the prism fills Nik's mind. She's worth more than Emma thinks. She deserves to speak up for herself.

'You heard me. You come here and complain about your life without so much as asking how I am. You never contact me unless you want something or need someone to talk to. Then, when you are here, you pass thinly veiled insults on our home, on our lives, our jobs, on us. I don't want to hear it anymore. You don't support your husband, you won't look after your own mother without whining about it, it's disgusting. I don't want someone like that in my house when all I've ever done is listen to you complain hour after hour and tried to be the listener you seem to want to use me as. I know you come here to make yourself feel superior, don't think I haven't noticed just because I'm too polite to say it. Not anymore. Get out. Take your demanding, careless nature with you.'

Nik's heart thunders in her chest as she waits for the stunned woman to make a retort. Will she be upset? Annoyed? Feel betrayed? Regret batters against the spire of confidence that surged in her, pulling away at its foundation brick by brick. Emma's face reddens just enough to notice, her brow knits together in incredulity over her ice blue eyes and her top lip draws into a sneer. She's chosen anger.

'Well, the true you finally shows herself, does she? I've always known you aren't the quiet, kind person you pretend to be. Then you come out with all that. How dare you. You of all people tell me that I don't support my family. What about you? You lounge around in bed for weeks on end. Depression? No, you're just lazy. You act the part when you feel like it and when you've had enough you switch on the sad face. Alastair deserves better than someone like you.

'You're right, coming here does make me feel better. I can't imagine living in such a house, in this area, having to work because my husband doesn't earn enough. It's unthinkable. I come here to remind myself that even though things aren't always easy I'm still lucky. There are plenty more out there like you who I can take my problems to, they're just sensible enough to see the benefits of having someone like me in their life. You're a bitch, Nikkita Walsh, and everyone will know it when I'm done.'

It isn't until the prism is out of Emma's hands that Nik is able to relax. She didn't hear most of what was said but fury rings in her ears. It isn't Nik who's showing her true colours. Each word that pours out of Emma's mouth validates every single one of Nikkita's, but her confidence still continues to crumble.

'Leave.' The quiver creeps into Nik's voice reluctantly, weakness washes over her.

'Gladly.'

Nik flinches as though Emma might spit at her on the way past. In fact it surprises her when she doesn't. She doesn't see Emma to the door. She doesn't jump when the picture frames rattle at its slamming. The prism is wrapped in her palm. One step after the another. Sinking into the corner spot on the sofa. Knees tucked up to her chest. It's the best position for crying.

# NINE
## *Nikkita*

Sometimes a good cry is all someone needs to calm down. For someone like Nik, who hates and actively avoids any kind of conflict, it helps immensely. When the tears stop falling and her heart stops shaking like her tightly clenched hands she takes a deep breath.

'I did the right thing. I had to stand up for myself. For Alastair. She can say what she wants about me, but not him. I actually stood up for myself. I've never done that before. Not like that. I didn't know I could.' She smiles. It's exhilarating to fight a battle on her own behalf. She hasn't looked at the prism since early morning. She doesn't want the image to become commonplace, but wants to reward her confidence. Unfurling her hands she twists the prism, raising it to one eye in happy anticipation. An anticipation that's quickly shattered.

The woman in the prism is ugly. More-so than she's ever pictured herself. Lifeless dank hair, a poor complexion, a long and miserable face with no shred of vitality or any emotions. Her face is old, body a little overweight, her clothes crinkled and dirty… but it's still her.

'This isn't right. This isn't Alastair's view. Where's his perception gone?' Whispers jab at her. "I do come here to make myself feel better. Alastair is never here to look after you. I can't imagine living in a house like this. You're a bitch Nikkita Walsh."

'Is this... Emma's perception? No, I don't want this, why am I seeing this? I want Alastair's back.' Panic drums a rhythm in her chest. 'Why did she have to ruin it? How am I supposed to feel beautiful without his help? Give it back to me!'

*You don't deserve to have it back. You upset Emma.*

'I do. I need it back.'

*You were horrible to her. Nasty and bitter. It's who you really are, you can't hide it anymore.*

'That's not who I am, she made me that way. I just couldn't stand it, what she was saying.'

*She came to you for help, she needed someone to talk to, and you threw her out. Maybe she was complaining because she needed to get things off her chest.*

'She was using me.'

*Maybe you were the only one who'd listen. She could have been vulnerable and not wanted to discuss her real problems.*

'Shut up.'

*Maybe she was lonely.*

'Stop it!'

*You were selfish. She was right about you.*

'…was she?'

*You are a bitch.*

It all knits together in her mind. The thoughts make sense. What if Emma really has no one else? What if the way she presents herself is a way of protecting herself too? And she turned her away… how could she disagree now? 'I'm... I'm horrible, OK. I should have let her stay. I feel awful for what I said to her. Maybe I do deserve her perception.'

*There's no maybe about it.*

She holds the prism, uselessness and acceptance rolling over like a blanket. A memory drifts back to her of the last time she'd come home from seeing Emma.

'You look knackered, Nik. What's wrong?' Alastair looked concerned.

'Oh, it's nothing just Emma is struggling with a few things…'

'Again?'

'Yeah.'

'What was it this time, the usual trivial stuff?' Alastair's dislike for Emma unintentionally seeps into the tone of his questions and responses.

'We shouldn't judge her. She just deals with things in different ways, she needed someone to listen.'

'Maybe no one's listening because she has nothing real to say.'

'Al.'

'Sorry, I know she's your friend but she only comes knocking on your door or message boxes when she needs something. You're too nice to ignore her, but I don't like seeing you get used like that.'

'Used? You think?'

'Yeah, I do. If you ask me you should stop meeting up with her. You need friends like Ellie who really care for you right now, not people who are willing to dump their complaints on you and nothing else. You matter too, Nik.'

He's right, she does matter. The negativity in her head is something she can push back against, however small the defence. She doesn't have to listen to it. It's no great speaker of truth. She'll figure out a way to get Alastair's gift back to normal.

*You'll never do it.*

'Shut up. I will. Because I matter too. I was right to ask Emma to leave. Maybe I wasn't right in all I said or how I said it, but I wasn't completely wrong. I'll figure it out.' There's no retort to hear in her head. Could that be the second battle she's won today?

The prism has closed again, and sits innocently enough in her hand. There has to be a way. Has the view in it changed because it's been touched by someone else? The memory of Emma staring at the prism with surprise and greed in her eyes flushes Nik with annoyance. Would she have pocketed it if she'd had more time? All her snobbery about not expecting them to own something nice. Just how long does your nose have to be to have such a judgmental view when looking at people down it? Ignore it and focus.

She turns the prism slowly, studying each triangular panel as she does. There has to be something. The colours have become dull, the blue as empty as the perception of her inside it. It no longer swirls or glitters in the sunlight. To open the prism she's always twisted it, but only one half and always the same way. Will it turn the opposite way as well? The panels on the 'top' of the prism have little golden tips so she can tell which way to hold and turn it. Taking it between her fingers she turns the prism the other way with caution. Fear of breaking it brings a sheen to her forehead.

It clicks on what she imagines are tiny gears within, and moves without resistance. A complex series of ticks and tacks sound and then the outer vibrancy of the colours returns. She looked at it a few minutes ago, and the warning not to view it more than once an hour looms in her mind. She doesn't understand why, but that's precisely the reason that she won't take the chance. Instead she'll use the next hour to calm right down, and search for some positivity. Hoping with everything she has that when she looks again she'll see Alastair's version of her.

It's the longest hour Nik has ever lived. The less she tries to think about the time, the louder the clock ticks. The prism sits in the sun where she can watch it sparkle, and she thinks only of the view she wants to return, calling the image beautiful and pretty in her head over and over and trying to overlay it on to the view she has of herself. Her palm shakes as the prism stands upon it, but when it opens she lets out a relieved sob and blinks away tears. The day at the beach is back, she fixed it! A deep fascination overtakes her. There has to be more to learn about the prism. She's unlocked one secret, and if there are others to discover she'll find them too.

# TEN
## *Alastair*

It takes Alastair a little while to find the restaurant his friend picked out. His knowledge of the city is non-existent, and he can only thank Google Maps for actually getting him here on time. A flicker of excitement zips around his stomach. He's looking forward to Ed's company. They used to have a good laugh due to his cocky nature, but he's the kind of person you can have serious conversations with when it counts. The restaurant is packed full, a good sign, and as he squints into the arrangement of tables he spots him. Edward looks well, a slight tan, still in trim condition. He was always a bit of a fitness buff. Does he have someone at home to care about too? He's swiping around on a large smartphone, but as soon as he sees Alastair his face spreads into a smile and he waves.

'Alastair.' They embrace briefly.

'Hey Ed, it's been a while.'

'It has, when did we last meet up? Last year?' Ed gestures for him to sit.

'Maybe even the year before I think. You were still back home then but you said you were moving soon. How do you like it here?'

'I love it, the bustle of the city is perfect for me. It's so much bigger than any cities at home.' They seat themselves and reach for menus, which they only half read. 'This place though, it's been my favourite restaurant since I got here. Was it far for you?'

'Nah, I'm at a city-centre hotel while I'm here on a business trip for a few months.'

'A few months, yeah you said.' Edward whistles. 'That's impressive, I bet it's half work, half relaxation in some penthouse suite right? Gotta reap the benefits of owning your own company.'

'I'd like a little less free time since I'm here for so long, but yeah the room they've put me in is pretty fancy. If I'd chosen myself I would have gone for something far more reasonable.'

'I'd be happy to take it off your hands.' He chuckles. Edward hasn't changed much since college, where they met. He still has a confidence about him that Alastair can't match. It rubs people the wrong way sometimes, but he'd grown into it as he got older and now has a fairly balanced personality. They had some mischievous times in their final year of study, but went to different universities after.

'What brings you out here, then? Are you living here permanently now with the job you mentioned?' Alastair reads through the menu properly while he asks.

'Nah, as much as I love it here I do miss home. I'm over scouting for places where we could set up a US office since the company is thinking of branching out in the next twelve months. So seems we were brought here for similar purposes. My stay here is long-term though, I think I've been out here six months already.'

'Wow, that's quite the long trip. Do you have someone at home?' A pang of longing for Nik chimed in the distance.

'A girlfriend? No, it seemed pointless while I'd still be travelling so much. Maybe when I'm back home and will actually be staying there for more than a year I'll start looking to settle, but for now I just take my fun where I can find it.' He flashes a cheeky wink.

Alastair smiles, but he'll take Nik over any fun that can be found in one night any day. Even though he acted like a bit of a player in college, Ed has never been disloyal to the girlfriends he's had. Yet now, and for a reason he can't pinpoint, Alastair wonders if that would still hold true.

'How's your missus doing?' As Ed asks the question Alastair bristles at the lack of the name.

'Nik? Things are OK, we moved into a new place a few years ago and it's a house we really wanted in a quieter area. Took a bit of fixing up but nothing major.'

'Have you got yourselves engaged yet?'

'No, not yet. We do want to get married, but when the time's right and when Nik is feeling better.' A waiter draws up to the table just as Edward's face fills with concern.

Crap, he's dropped himself in it there.

They order their choices and drinks and wait for the hovering serviceman to speed away to tend to other tables. Change the subject! 'Tell me about your company's plan to expand, it's a big step to move into a new market. What was your business again, real estate? It's a whole different game over here.' For now Edward respects the topic change, and is more than happy to talk shop with someone who owns their own company.

Ed is doing well, but he isn't his own boss. Alastair can tell that he very much wants to be. The life seeps back into him as he socialises. To not be in a hotel room worrying about Nik and watching unfamiliar television shows feels wonderfully alien. He didn't intend to mention that Nik is unwell. Apart from one friend he hasn't told anyone of her struggles. It seems a betrayal to discuss her with others. His hopes that Ed would forget what he said are dashed, though. The food is fantastic and near the end of the meal, with both men in good spirits, Ed asks the dreaded question.

'So what did you mean? When you said you'll get married when Nik gets better? Is everything alright?'

Alastair battles back a sigh, it feels wrong to refute the question when Ed only seems concerned.

'Nik... has been unwell for a while. It's not all the time, it's just on and off, but it's a constant struggle.' The amber liquid swirls in his glass idly as he speaks.

'Is it something serious? She's not terminally ill, is she?' Why is that always the assumption people jump to?

'Oh, no, no nothing like that, sorry I didn't mean to give that impression. She's not physically ill, but she struggles with serious intermittent depression. I'm really not sure how to help her with it, but I try and do what I can.'

'Depression? So she just gets really sad sometimes?'

A momentary flare of irritation pokes Alastair in the chest. 'I know that's what people think depression is, but it's much more than that. Sometimes she's in bed for days, she can't get up or do anything.'

'Sounds like she just needs to get out of the house a bit, clear the cobwebs away.' Another jab by the finger that doesn't understand. 'She's got nothing to be sad about from where I'm sitting.' Poke. Where has his haughty air of dismissal come from?

'It's not about having things to be sad about, sometimes it comes along for no reason. You're not being very fair here, Ed.'

'I don't mean any offense, it's just that depression is down to the person who's ill. They have control of their own minds, it's up to them whether they stay sad or somehow cheer themselves up.'

The jabbing of accusation becomes more forceful. He has to keep calm. Maybe Ed has changed after all… and not for the better.

'That's a very skewed view.'

'I just have a different outlook on it. So many people now complain about depression, people even take days off work for it and I just don't get it. Being sad does nothing to stop you sitting at a desk and getting on with things.'

Now the finger stays, pressing and burning at the centre of his chest. 'I've already said it's more than just feeling sad. It doesn't sound like you know the first thing about depression or looking after someone who has it.' *Keep your cool, Alastair. He doesn't know what it's like, you've heard these misconceptions before. Just keep calm.*

'What looking after could she need? You make it sound debilitating.'

The fire catches on his skin, radiating out. Mingling with the grieving disappointment of his friend's stance. 'It is, when it hits hard.'

'Sounds like a whole lot of bother to me. You sound like her carer. Why not just go out there and find someone normal, someone easier to live with who can make you happy instead of dragging you down with them?'

Alastair is engulfed by the flames now, all-consumed. Clearly he hasn't managed to stop it showing on his face, because Ed's eyes widen and shift back and forth. He can't stop the contempt pouring out in his response.

'Firstly,' Alastair's voice is low and dangerous, 'I would never leave Nik just because she isn't well at times. Secondly, depression is a serious condition that you know nothing about. So before you go spewing opinions on how depressed people are just sad or they're lazy because they don't go to work you might want to inform yourself about it a bit more. Nik has no more control over her illness than someone with any other disease or disability, but she works damn hard to fight her way out of it and to not let it control her. People can't be strong every minute of every day. Third, I will look after her every single day if she needs it. It's my privilege to be her partner and one day her husband, and unlike people like you who's outlook has disappointed me, I can see past her illness and think she's a wonderful person who I'm happy to be there for. I think this meal is over.'

'Alastair don't, I didn't mean to upset you.'

'It's too late to backtrack.' Shaking hands fiddle with his wallet and he leaves enough to cover his share of the bill on the table. Edward makes to get up. 'Don't. I don't want your company at the moment.' His friend's face sags, heavy with hindsight. There are probably one hundred apologies stuck in his throat, but Alastair doesn't want to hear them. He's too angry for it, too offended on Nik's behalf and disappointed in someone he's always liked.

To have to sit there and be told he should leave Nik because of something like depression, something she can't help and fights so hard to cope with, is too much. Did he defend her well? The rush of the busy roads and streets only makes him feel more claustrophobic as he strides out of the restaurant and in the direction he guesses will take him back to his hotel.

How had that meal gone south so fast? He'd been enjoying himself, glad of the company. When did Ed become that shallow? Has he always been that way and Alastair just never noticed? He thought he heard Ed shouting for him to return to the table as he left, but can't be sure. He has to walk, it doesn't matter where. Walk until all the anger in him drains away. The more he walks, the more it works. It leaves him, spilling into the streets like a trail of water from a punctured balloon. By the time he has to consult his phone to check where he is he's utterly deflated. Why can't people have some compassion? Why can't they look past what people have and see who they really are. Depression is a part of Nik, he accepts that and wants to help, but it doesn't define her. Why can't other people see that too?

There's only one friend he knows of that would be able to calm him down, but they haven't spoken for a while and he doesn't want to just drop in with his problems so unannounced. He'll message Luke tomorrow, see how he's doing. Just speaking to someone, anyone other than Edward, will be a welcome distraction. Perhaps he can lose himself in catching up on his friend's life and happenings. Yet here's the guilt again. He should keep in contact with Luke more regularly and not just when he needs a chat himself. He isn't far from the hotel, and when he returns to his room all he intends to do is sleep.

# ELEVEN
## *Nikkita*

*I know how it works now, I have it all figured out. There's so much more to it than I imagined. I've solved it.* Nikkita is sitting on the sofa. She's barely moved since she figured out that the prism might do more than just show one perception. That was two days ago. She's still in the same clothes, her hair unkempt from sleeping downstairs and not being brushed or washed. Her knees ache from being tucked up close to her, and her eyes sting from scouring the surface of the prism for any small sign of controls.

Most of its functions have been unlocked by turning it in various combinations, like some kind of delicate triangular Rubik's cube. The colours on the outside often change as she experiments, but she always knows how to return to the deep and glittering blue that signals Alastair's view. She never breaks any of the rules. Never looks more than once an hour, and doesn't look at all if she's feeling negative about herself. She doesn't need the rules anymore, they are ingrained in her mind and body. She's forged a connection with the prism. She understands it and it trusts her. Why else would it allow all of its secrets to be discovered?

'It trusts me. It wants me to understand it and now I do. There's so much possibility. I have to do some experiments, but where should I start?' It's comforting to speak aloud, throwing something, anything into the silent void of the empty house. She's ignorant of the slight manic edge to her voice though, the strain in it. Obsession has kept tiredness away, but now her tasks are complete it presses in upon her. 'I should sleep upstairs tonight, have a shower. When did I last eat? Doesn't really matter, might help me shift a bit of weight, but Alastair wouldn't like that. What experiments can I do? Who can I use to see? Who would be free to meet up at this time in the evening? No one. I'll make a start tomorrow. I have to collect them, the perceptions of people who like me. I have to fill the prism with anything other than Emma's view. If Alastair's view helped me that much, so can everyone else's, right? I'll only get them from people I already know. People who love me. I'll message Ellie and see if she's available this week. Surely she doesn't see me negatively, not when she understands me so well.' She reaches for her phone. Messages from Alastair sit unanswered for longer than usual. He'll worry if she doesn't reply soon.

When all the notifications are gone, all the messages answered, she contacts Ellie to see if she's free at the weekend. Guilt pokes at her heart as she messages. Ellie is always so busy that Nik usually waits for her to get in contact and doesn't want to bother her, but she needs her, and not just to try out her theory with the prism.

A thought scuttles across her mind like an insidious insect.

*I could find more.*

*What about the strangers? How do they see you? Someone you've never met before. Isn't that a better way to judge how you really look?*

*Maybe.*

*Think about it, you have the power to collect the perception of as many people as you want.*

*I don't know that. I don't know how many the prism can hold.*

*Why not try and find out? You're supposed to know all of its secrets aren't you? Everything about it? How can you be truly connected to it when there are still things you don't know?*

*I don't need the perceptions of everyone. I just want some of people who actually like me to go alongside Al's.*

*You're being selfish. Shouldn't you balance it? Instead of being vain and only going for those you know will be good. The ones you hope are good. They could all hate you too, they could all think you're ugly. The question is whether a total stranger will hate you within seconds. Then you'll know if you really are someone that can't be loved or liked. Don't you want to know the answer to that?*

*Why would someone want to know that?*

*You have the power to find out. To answer a question people can only wonder about. It would be foolish not to use it. Use the gift to its full extent, complete your bond with it, unlock every... little... secret.*

*I will... I'll find out the truth. I'll start with Ellie though, because she'll understand.*

*You can't tell her about the prism and what it does.*

*I know. It's my little secret.*

The weekend rolls around fast and Nik brims with happy little bubbles. She's grateful that Ellie is free to meet up, and as she heads over to their usual haunt she can't help but smile. The city is busy, as expected, but Ellie is already there and waiting at their favourite table. She looks amazing as always. A twang of jealousy writhes as Nik thinks of her own casual clothing ensemble and hair shoved back into a ponytail. What is someone like her doing sitting with someone like Ellie?

'Nik!' Ellie trots over to give a genuine hug, squeezing Nik gently as she returns the gesture. 'I'm sorry it's been a while since we met, I'm so glad you messaged me!' Her energy is both unbelievable and infectious. Smile so wide that it passes to those around her at times. What Nik wouldn't give to borrow just a little of it.

'You weren't too busy?'

'Not for you. I got you a hazelnut latte like always, and I won't hear the slightest suggestion of you giving me the money either. Not this time.'

Nik considers protesting, but they always end up

bickering about the bill in a loving way, so she opts straight for compromise. 'I'll get the next one then. Thank you. How are you?'

'I'm great, things are going well with work for both of us, we had an offer accepted on our dream house so we just need our sale to complete. Luckily the new house isn't far away from the old one so it shouldn't be too much of a hassle.'

'That's amazing, please let us know if you need any help with the move, OK? And please tell me you have pictures?'

'I was hoping you'd ask!' They sit together and chat about anything and everything that comes to mind. Ellie's shiny, long brown hair makes her every expression even more animated. Her high cheek bones and bright blue eyes need no make-up. Even with Alastair's view she can't admit to being prettier than Ellie. Over an hour passes and Nik takes her turn ordering their drinks, and when she sits back down the change in subject looms like a change in temperature when a window is opened on a cold day.

'So how are you really, Nik? You know I always ask more than once because you tend to say "I'm OK" or "I'm fine" by default.'

Being transparent is hard. Between Al and Ellie it's a wonder Nik isn't made of glass. Maybe she is, she does sometimes feel she might shatter. 'I'm... better than I was. It's just hard at the moment...'

'Oh yeah, you said Alastair is off on business again.' Nik nods into her cup. 'How long this time?'

'Three months. He's negotiating the acquisition of a new company in America.'

'Why didn't you tell me? You didn't say he was away for that long. I could have come over.'

'No it's alright, I have to look after myself. I can't keep relying on you for company. I'd love it if you came to visit soon, but I have to sort myself out. I'm a grown woman, I should be able to live alone for a little while.'

'Stop reasoning it away, it's perfectly valid to feel sad and lonely about it.' There it is, the kind of understanding she so needs at that moment. Justification. 'I'll definitely make time to come over soon, we can have a girly weekend like old times. How are you keeping yourself busy?'

The presence of the prism in Nik's pocket becomes so obvious it could have burned a hole through it.

'I've just been pottering around the house, doing little bits and bobs. I've done some work, though probably not enough. Just before he went... I really wasn't all that well, so I'm trying not to fall back into that now he's away.'

'Well look at what you've achieved today, you came out to meet me, so you're winning the fight this time.' They both smile.

'I wish it felt more like I was winning something.' Nik stares at the swirling browns of her coffee, when would it start to feel she was winning?

'You're so brave. Please don't forget that. You fight so hard just to feel the way many people take for granted.'

'You've fought it too.' *And you did a much better job kicking its ass than I do.*

'I did, so many people do. We aren't alone, half the people in this cafe are probably struggling.' Ellie's words are true enough. Nik knows there are many like herself who are masters of the masquerade. Looking at them in passing you assume nothing is wrong, that they're confident and living the life they want. Humans have become emotional chameleons. That's why people don't trust each other anymore. You never know what mask they're wearing, or what's buried beneath. It's time to lift Ellie's mask. Nik takes a deep breath before speaking.

'Alastair got me a gift before he left.'

'Awww, he's so sweet. I wish Brad was a bit more like him. I love him, don't get me wrong, but he isn't as thoughtful as Alastair.'

'I'm lucky to have him, I really don't understand what he sees in me.'

'You don't have to understand it, you just have to accept it.'

The words strike a chord with Nik. She always pushes back against the lovely things Alastair says about her because she doesn't believe they're true. It's such a simple idea. She doesn't have to believe them, she just has to accept them. To accept him. 'So what did he get you?'

Nik reaches into her pocket. 'This little ornament, like a good luck charm. He says if I keep it with me it will remind me of him and take away all my sad feelings.' Lying to Ellie turns her stomach, though it isn't a complete lie, but she can't tell her its true function. Who would believe her?

'Wow, can I see?'

Her stomach flutters, it's going to take her perception. 'Sure.' Only Nik hears the hum start up over the chittering drone of socialisation in the cafe.

'It's so beautiful, look at the colours. Where did he get it?'

'He said it was from a quirky little gift shop on the outskirts of the city. He must have put so much effort in to finding something like this.'

'I'll say, I've never seen a shop that sells this kind of thing. And he said it's meant to make you feel better?'

'I think it's probably more meant to be a comfort than an actual working thing.' Another lie.

'You never know, it could be made with some of those mood stone things, some people swear by them when it comes to actually making people feel better.'

'Maybe, I hadn't thought of that. It makes me think of him and that's all I need.'

The colour shifts slightly. It's done. It's siphoned what it needs.

*Look at you, you can't wait to get home and see. Itching like a girl in a tub of spiders. You should have more respect for your friend. You don't trust her, that's why you had to use the prism on her.*

*That's not true, I trust her. I trust Ellie more than anything, and that's why I'm using the prism, because I know I'll find a good version of myself in her.* But the thought isn't wrong, she does want to get home. To sit on the sofa, the place where she discovered the secrets of the prism, and view the truth of her friend's perception. She pushes it down, forcing it away, so that she can continue to enjoy her time with Ellie.

'He'll propose to you next.' *That's laughable. Who would propose to me?* 'I bet you this time next year you'll be engaged.' Ellie's face was so full of determination that Nik almost believed her words… but not quite.

'I don't think so. We talked about it but he wants me to be a little better first.'

'You are better, at least a lot better than you were a few years ago. I don't think your illness would stop him from marrying you in the slightest. Was it your idea or his that you want to be better first?'

Nik thinks about it. 'It was… mine. I'd forgotten. I thought he just wasn't ready yet.'

'See, he's probably been ready for a while, but he's not the kind of person to pressure you. He wants to make sure you're ready and well, too. Do you want to be Mrs Nikkita Deene?'

'I do. It would mean the world. I'd be proud to call him my husband.' They smile, there had been no hesitation.

'You two are so cute. Do I get to come to the wedding?'

'Are you kidding, you'd be maid of honour, right up there at the front with me.' Emotion fills them both.

'You'll make such a beautiful bride Nik, and a great wife.'

*She's lyin-*
*Shut up!*

And to Nik's surprise the negative voice does shut up.

A feeling of power floods through her. She's stronger than it. She's in control. She often feels this way after meeting with Ellie. Her friend's belief in her is fortifying.

'What about you, when do you think Brad will propose?'

'Oh I don't know, that could be years away. He's in project mode with the house and everything and you know what he's like with money.' As they resume their chatterboxing, the urge to go home and view the prism fades like a sun-bleached stain. She wants to stay right here with Ellie. Talking about anything and everything. Being able to air her troubles and being met with nothing but understanding and validation. It's OK to feel the way she does. It's OK not to be OK. She's safe here. It's OK to be Nikkita here, she's welcomed and protected in one. If she could stay in the cafe with Ellie and talk her troubles away for days then she would.

# TWELVE
## *Nikkita*

After the bustle of the cafe the quiet of the house is deafening. It fascinates Nik how people will meet in such public places to discuss all sorts of personal problems, but over time she's realised why. Places like city centre cafes are so very public that they become private in their own right. There are so many people there that you yourself don't matter. So many problems collecting in a cloud and drifting high above their owners that yours are lost among them in an expulsion too crowded to distinguish. Everyone is so absorbed in their talking that you can say anything and it'll disappear among the cacophonous chatter of everyday life. There's something comforting about that.

Nik is lighter after talking with Ellie. Every time without fail. She doesn't need to put on a façade. There's no need to be guilty about her feelings, because Ellie understands. It's validating and such a relief to speak with someone without being judged. As awareness of the prism in her pocket returns, it seems like a betrayal to even consider looking at it.

'Do I really want to know what Ellie thinks of me? What if she doesn't like me at all? Why isn't feeling better after talking to her enough?' An insect wriggles around in her mind, what if the only other person besides Alastair to understand her sees her the way Emma does.

'There's only one way to find out. I'm not doing anything wrong.'

*Why didn't you just ask her? Tell her the truth about the prism instead of sneaking around behind her back?*

Would Ellie have believed it? Nik considers it. Ellie would do anything in her power to help Nik, and if she told her that the prism captures the view of the person holding it she probably would have held out her hand, ready to help without question. Had the sneaking been pointless?

'I had to. I think she would've humoured me, but I'm not sure she'd believe I had a magic prism in my pocket. She would have held it like I asked, but I know how weird it sounds. I wouldn't want to worry her. I wouldn't want to taint the image she gave either. If she knew she was doing it to help me she might have imagined me differently. I need the truth. I'm going to look.' Her hands shake, what if the prism hasn't captured what it needed to, or she accidentally opens it on Emma's perception? She hasn't figured out how to remove perceptions yet, but she will. She's bound to the prism now, it's sharing its secrets with her, but there's more to learn. The sofa dips as she settles into the hollow space her body has made. The cushions fit around her perfectly, a mould of herself to slip in to. The prism is still swirling with blue, that's Alastair's view. She thinks back to the colour it turned when Ellie held it in her hand, and twists the bottom half until that colour shows. As the viewing panel drops, a drawbridge to the truth, she lifts the prism to her eye.

Nik blinks away the tears that form, so the image doesn't smudge. There's not much time to look. She's pretty again, but in a different way than Alastair sees her. As she watches herself sit down at the cafe table her shiny, sandy-blonde hair falls over one shoulder in its little ponytail. Her face has a subtle beauty to it despite her wearing no make-up, and her casual clothes compliment a figure she only dreams of having. Snatches of thoughts caress her mind. They come in Ellie's voice along with a twisting of the stomach, it's only small and there's no malice in it.

*"She looks so pretty today. I wish I looked like her. I have to work on myself for hours to look half-decent. Nik doesn't even need make-up. She makes casual clothes look smart too with that figure. If I wear casual clothes I look like a bag of potatoes. I wish she could see it."*

*Is this... jealousy? Ellie is jealous of me? Ellie is so stunning, how could someone like her possibly want to look like someone as plain as me?*

The image fades, lost for another hour. Nik brims from head to toe as though she might burst. Her tears are happy ones. There are two now, two perceptions that prove her wrong. Does it mean she isn't right about herself after all? She tries to overlay her own perception on to theirs, and still can't see it entirely, but now little parts of what her partner and friend see are visible.

*You're kidding yourself if you think they aren't lying. The prism is a trick, one Alastair fashioned to make you happy so he doesn't have to deal with your miserable face. Ellie is in on it too.*

*Shut up, you're the liar here. The prism isn't a trick, it's the truth. I have two perceptions now, two that differ from the one you gave me.*

*You'll never escape my perception of us. You told me what we look like, you gave me all the power. Too much power. Two measly perceptions isn't going to change what we are.*

*It will. I have their support now. I've always had it, I've just been too blind to see what it meant. Alastair has always believed I was beautiful, it was you who pushed him away, and me who let you. Not now though. Now I've seen the truth with my own eyes I won't block it out. I'll accept it, and I'll fight you every step of the way. I may be the one who gave you your power over me, but that means I can take it away just as easily. I'm in control, not you. You won't win anymore.*

She waits for a response that never comes, and victory melds with love for Alastair and Ellie to form a feeling she's rarely known... confidence.

# THIRTEEN
## The Space Between

There's no lack of light, but it doesn't seem to travel all that far. Black plains roll far and wide, devoid of lustre. It's not entirely flat, but there are no beacons or paths to mark the way. It's fortunate that this is a place rarely travelled by those with a need to find the way out. At the epicentre of the space a speck sits in solitude, surrounded by emptiness. There's no wind, but for the whispering zephyrs that dart around. No sky from which rain might fall, just a white expanse bleached clean of colour. For all its wealth of space it's home to a single soul, which crouches next to a large, rock-ringed pond. It runs deep, near-endless, reaching down into depths rarely travelled, at least not by those who choose to live.

The pond's boundary is clearly marked. People would know not to enter it by the dangerous glint of the treacle-smooth surface. There are no provisions for survival, just a hunched figure planted on a boulder at the pond-side. Its eyes dart back and forth, glaring at the high-flying flashes that descend and dive when they dare. The figure is harried, but ready to strike again with the rock it holds in its hand. Glistening fragments of reflective glass litter the boulder and black sand around it.

'Goddamn mirrorbirds, nothing but a nuisance.' It

mutters to itself in total comfort, content to be alone and solely responsible for the place it guards. 'Ever since she got that damn prism they've been relentless. I'll be damned if I let them form together. I've no shortage of rocks.' Another bird takes a dive, flanked by those encouraged by its boldness. They swarm the figure, corralling it in distraction while its partners flutter together inches from the water. They swoop so close that the whistle of flying glass resonates in the empty space. 'Give it up, clear off! This is my pond, I don't want you making unwanted friends for me.' Waving the birds away it slaps at one, stunning it and crushing it under a heel on the edge of the boulder. The others tweet crystal notes in mourning and take back to the sky. The rock launched from its hand strikes the flittering group and drops into the water. It floats, against common belief, and bobs on the surface for several minutes before small liquid hands drag it and the injured bird away. Down and down and down they go, disappearing into the vertical abyss. Not so much as a ripple remains.

Nikkita has become stronger lately. Its hold is swaying, its power less impactful. As it leans over the pond it sniggers as it catches a glimpse of its face on the sheet of water. 'Her perception of herself hasn't improved that much if I'm still this ugly.' A cruel laugh chokes the silence. The figure shares a name with the object of its malice, but will not be called by it. If you ask its name, it will say "call me Nothing, for that's what I'm worth". Nothing looks up, sighing at the renewed flock of mirrorbirds. Is there no end to them? They descend together, knowing there are too many of them to be shooed away by the angry squatter. 'This place is mine, she gave it to me, why can't they leave me be and let me do my work in peace?'

They swarm on the opposite side of the pond this time, not bothering to distract it, and pack themselves tighter and tighter together. 'Stop that!' Nothing rises, bolting to the collaboration in the hopes of breaking it up. They're too fast. They begin to link together like a sculpture puzzle, and when enough pieces have attached to each other a panic crosses Nothing's greasy face. 'I said stop!' It's too late. Too formed. The screeching of glass makes Nothing flinch as it searches for a way to halt the process. 'The pond, I can push it in,' and so it does. Ignoring the sharp scrape of the jagged edges against the skin of its palms. Watching it topple, aided by the rocky outline of the pond, a victorious laugh barks out but only briefly.

Mirrored wings burst from the still-shaping clod of glass and lift it above the surface of the pond before it meets its shimmering touch. Nothing scrambles back to the boulder, it will claim it as its own if it has to. It doesn't want any company, it wants sole dominion. The figure takes a more and more definite shape, and a flicker grows in Nothing's chest. 'She's come this far in so short a time? Shit. How strong will the new one be?' The wings plant the new figure safely on the shore of the opposite side of the pond. Colour seeps into it and gives it life, the opposite of Nothing who lives in monotonal greys, whites and blacks. When it finally speaks and the light around it fades, Nothing can only scowl at its new companion.

'Well, this is rather a grim place isn't it? Could you do anything to brighten it up?' The new apparition's bright blue eyes are stark against the black land and white sky.

'Why would I need something as pointless as colour? This is my home and I like it the way it is.'

'Don't you think we should introduce ourselves? It would only be polite.'

'I have no need of manners, or the likes of you.'

'Feisty. Well, I'm Nikkita. Should I call you that, too?'

'No, you can call me Nothing. That's what she's worth.'

Anger creases her otherwise faultless face. 'She's worth a great deal, and if she believes otherwise it's only because of your games and meddling. Why do you punish her the way you do?'

'Because she created me for that purpose and gave me control.'

'Obviously you don't have that much power anymore, else I wouldn't exist.'

Nothing looks her up and down. There's no denying that this Nikkita is an improvement on itself. Her figure more toned, clear complexion and shiny hair that falls a few inches past her shoulders with a natural beauty. It fights off the stab of longing, of jealousy, that sparks more anger.

'You're a lie. Placed by Alastair to make her feel better. He doesn't really see her that way, he just doesn't want to deal with her being miserable anymore.'

'I'm not only his view, I'm Ellie's view too. I'm a new perception, and you won't continue to be the only one with influence over her.' Nikkita begins to stroll around the pond.

'Back off, I don't want you near me.'

'You don't own this pond anymore.'

'Get back, this is my home.'

'You've been alone for a very long time, isn't that painful?'

'Shut up!' Nothing throws a rock, but Nikkita catches it with ease.

'You cut your hands when you tried to push me in to the pond, let me see, I can help you.' With wide eyes Nothing scrambles away, kicking and scraping against the boulder it sits on.

'Don't come NEAR ME!' It's scared. Of what? Of kindness? Nikkita halts, struck in the arm by another rock. To push it will be dangerous.

'Alright.' She takes a step backward. 'What do you say to half each? I won't come over there, and you don't come over to my side unless you want to.'

Nothing relaxes and moves back to its spot on the boulder. Seething eyes burn, stoked by the fear of contact, of caring. What a pitiful being it is to be unknowing of the kindness of others.

'As long as you don't come that close to me again, I don't care what you do. You don't deserve to be here.'

'I'll make myself comfortable.' Nikkita ignores the negative comment. 'You won't have a hold on her for much longer, you know. She's breaking free of you.'

'She's mine. She always will be. We've been together too long to be separated now. You don't get to come here and shout the odds. You know nothing about Nikkita. She doesn't need you, she needs me. I've kept her safe for years.'

'Kept her safe? That's what you call it? You've kept her down. Trodden her confidence into the ground and buried it under mounds of negative sand. You've drained her of any love she could have for herself. Everyone deserves to feel beautiful and worthy at some point in their lives and you, you're sitting here stewing in your own hate and fear and taking that away from her.'

'Oh? And if she felt beautiful what then? If she had confidence, what then? Someone would come along and tell her she's ugly, like they did when she was younger, and she'll be heartbroken. She was heartbroken. You weren't here the day I was born, but I heard the thoughts she had, the things the high school kids said. If I make sure she thinks she's ugly, then nothing will hurt her, nothing will surprise her, there will be nothing that can be said that she doesn't already know about herself. Look at me, I'm what she believes she is.'

'I see you, and I see your selfishness. You're spouting bullshit here, Nothing. You enjoy the power you have over her. You enjoy arguing with her about the truth, twisting her mind in favour of your negative tendencies. You feed off it, get your power from it, and you don't like it now that she's seeing some other way. I won't let you continue. She won't let you continue. We'll stop you.'

'You can try.' Crooked teeth decorate a malicious smile. 'Seems you're not stupid. You can see through me. I almost respect that. You have a little more power than I expected, but it won't last long. She won't continue to believe it. She plans to collect more perceptions, and trust me, when the next negative one comes along she will cling to it. It's what people do. No matter how much good happens to them, or is said to them, they always linger on the negative things. Even if it's only one. Even if it's only small. That's what they dwell on.

'I'll make sure she doesn't ignore the next bad perception. I'll make sure she doesn't continue to believe in your truth. You'll fade away, or I'll crush you, like the many mirrorbirds I crushed before you.'

Nothing scoops up a handful of black sand and glass and tightens its grip on it. A twisted smile adorns its face as the shards of glass press into its palms and draw dark grey blood. So many façades to see through, so much to decipher. Nothing about Nothing is true. It's scared, lonely, but stuck in its ways and dependent on Nikkita. New Nik will have to change that.

# FOURTEEN
## Alastair

It's only as he looks at the date on his work calendar that Alastair realises he's already been away from home for a month. The bed is strewn with papers, files and the laptop. They spill over onto every surface. He sits among them, cross-legged, reading a thick volume of new, and in part unwelcome, negotiation terms from the company he's working towards acquiring. Their skittishness isn't because they are nervous about the merger, it's because they are nervous about him discovering that they've sought further legal advice and completely altered their terms of sale and every other aspect of the deal. As he scours the contract, taking in everything they want to propose, and the list of all his original terms they want to reject or modify, the impulse to throw the dossier across the room and just go home simmers under his surface.

*I didn't ask for this. I know I asked to be the owner of my own business, and I wanted to reach out to merge with this company, but it was meant to be a simple deal. We didn't ask for anything ridiculous, they agreed to everything over the phone, then dragged me out here and went back on all of it. It makes sense why they wanted me here for so long now.*

He puts the bulky document down, leaving his pen between the pages to mark his place and lies back, trying not to crease any of the surrounding papers. He lifts a few to look for his lost phone, but gives up. In the back of his mind he knows he received a message a few minutes ago, or was it an hour ago? He's spoken with Luke regularly since the night of the dinner with Ed, and they've been messaging back and forth tonight as well until he picked up this damn document. He'll have to answer the message later.

He's become quite familiar with the ceiling of his hotel room. Every speck and inconsistent bump in the paint. He wants his own ceiling, the one in his bedroom in their home, where he knows if he looks sideways he'll see Nik sleeping next to him. It's too late to call her now because of the time difference, she'll be out for the count, but it doesn't stop him longing for it.

The wheels in his mind turn anticlockwise, taking him back into the annals of his memory as he wonders if he's done the right thing. Lived his life the right way.

*I could just ignore these documents and go to sleep. Turn off my work phone, shut down my computer, shove everything off the bed and relax. Then tomorrow I could walk out of here and head straight to the airport. In less than a day I could be home, holding Nik in my arms. If they're pushing back this hard do we really need the merger? Maybe I've been greedy? My business does so well at home, perhaps I should be happy with that. I just... want to do well, but maybe I already do and haven't noticed. When will it be enough for her approval?*

Comments from his mother swirl in his mind in a merry-go-round of dismissal.

"You'll never achieve anything, I didn't, your lousy

father didn't, and you won't neither. We don't 'ave money, and we'll never be the type of people that do. The world will take one look at you and laugh in your face, time you started accepting that now. Make yourself some dinner, I'm off down the pub." He'd been around fourteen then, and told his mother he wanted to be a businessman and wear a suit with smart creases in the legs and a tie and suit jacket. She barely looked after him, and he suspected as he got older that she didn't want him having any fancy notions about getting out of her house. Underneath all the harshness and distance she forced between them, she was scared he would leave her like his dad left her. She was lonely and sad, and he only wished he'd known sooner. He didn't realise until it was too late, and they grew apart too much to make things right.

'Are you watching me, Mum? Are you proud? You said I'd have nothing, only showed any interest in it when you realised I was making good profit. Then you slipped away and no one called me to tell me because my number wasn't in your phone or phonebook. Is this enough? I have a house, a woman I want to marry, a career... everything you said I couldn't do or have. I'm glad I became more than you told me I would.'

He worries his sadness might leak from him and soak the strewn papers. He's grateful for everything he has, there's no mistaking it, but sometimes he doesn't want it. Days like today. Sometimes he wants no business, no responsibility. Thinking back to what Edward said, and his reaction to his words, his chest tightens. He defended Nik, of course he did and always would, but he heard in Ed things that crept across his own mind from time to time.

Sometimes he doesn't want a partner who's depressed. Sometimes he wants Nik to be magically cured, to go back to being the woman he first met. Sometimes he wants a different Nik than the one he's come to discover. Not all the time. Not even most of the time. He doesn't always feel capable of caring for her, doubt is just as normal for him. Why is that something to feel guilty about? Why shouldn't he wish for better times for them both?

He thought things would get better for her after she made the move to the career she really wanted. Working in an office environment was making her much worse. It was a petty office where the politics were everything and the career ladder short and missing a lot of rungs. There was nothing but snide remarks and subtext and people reading too much into things. Her own manager had even told her she needed to appear happy all the time, even on days she didn't feel it, despite knowing she struggled with depression. That was the day Alastair told her she never had to go back there. The day he told her she would set up the freelance business she'd always wanted, and would never have to work for people like that manager again. She'd been hesitant, concerned about the time it would take to build up clients and her lack of financial contribution. He would hear none of it. He doesn't brag about it, but his earnings are more than enough for the both of them to live on. He peels himself off of the bed and stands at the balcony window.

*I don't regret supporting her. She's made a good strong client list. I just don't think either of us thought about the fact she'd be alone so much. I couldn't do it, work at home all day every day, I know that much. She needs it, though. That way if she's feeling down she can rest in bed, she's not beholden to any idiot managers anymore, she's free. Of that at least.*

Her mind is so complex, what would it be like to see how she sees the world? For all her over-thinking and practicalities and endless organisational lists to stop her worrying he's never met someone with a more beautiful mind, even when it was clogged with that dark fog. Her kindness spreads beyond boundaries, her consideration for others often present in everything she does. Birthdays are never forgotten, anniversaries, appointments for either him or her, all of it stored safely in her head. She has so much to give, and that's why he hates depression. It traps and pollutes her mind and makes her feel inadequate. He can't do anything. It's the most infuriating feeling in the world.

He fights back tears as he stares out into the darkening city-scape. The trilling, obnoxious tinker of an old phone blares from the speakers of his mobile. His work one. It's Derek, he'd only call this late on business. He's been reading the contract through too, hopefully he hasn't found anything bad. 'At this hour? For fuck sake, he's on the next floor down why didn't he just come up? At least then I'd have some company.' With a tired reluctance he picks up the phone, getting rid of his annoyed sigh before he answers. He just wants some peace and quiet.

# FIFTEEN
## Alastair

The knock at the hotel room door comes to Alastair through a fog of deep sleep. Why can't people just leave him alone? The phone, emails, and now knocking on the door at this time? Wait... what is the time? Panic puppets him out of bed, leaving his consciousness to drag itself out of slumber at a slower pace. *Did I oversleep? Am I late for a meeting? Did something happen with the negotiations? What time is it?* The light from his phone screen plunges into his drowsy eyes, and through squinting lids he sees shaky numbers that orient him. It's nine o'clock, but underneath is the date, and it's a Saturday. *Saturday... so who's at my door?* Another round of knocking ensues and he is both ashamed and glad to notice that he slept fully clothed.

'Just a sec, hold on.' Whoever it is, they aren't expected. He stumbles towards the window and throws the curtains open. Various non-sensical ideas rush through his lethargic mind. *Something's happened to Nik and the hotel staff are coming to tell me. Maybe Nik flew out here, no don't be silly, go and open the door.* When he does, his jaw drops in shock like a stunned goldfish.

'Still in bed at nine? When did you become such a slob?'

'Luke! What are you doing here? When did you get here?'

'I drove up last night after our talk on What's App, you didn't sound too good. I wanted to make sure you were OK.'

The unanswered message Alastair meant to reply to drifts back to mind. He didn't mean to cause concern. 'You drove all the way here from home? That's like... a six hour drive!'

'I made it in five and a half.' Luke flashes a cheeky wink. 'I was gonna ask anyway if you wanted to meet this month while you're here, like we talked about, but I invited myself along. You gonna leave me on your doorstep?'

'I... n-no of course not, I'm just surprised.'

'A good surprise, I hope?'

'It so is, sorry I'm not quite awake yet. Excuse the state of the room.' He ushers Luke in with a beaming smile, he's never been happier to see him.

'Christ Al, what happened in here? Did a document bomb go off? I can see where you slept between the papers.'

'Work's been busy, I was reading over the negotiation stuff last night. You know the drill, anything you see is confidential.'

'I wonder what people would say if they found out I know all your company's little secrets.' Luke smiles playfully. He's been to Luke for advice before about the company. Luke used to be a high-powered businessman living the stressful life of a London executive, but it got the better of him and he moved away. Out of the city, out of the country, and works for himself as an adviser to growing companies from a huge and gorgeous home surrounded by land, peace and quiet, and a lovely family. Alastair always thought Luke got out just in time, before the stress gave him a heart attack or stroke, and he couldn't be more glad that he'd changed his lifestyle. Luke surveys the mess of papers and shoves his hands into his jean pockets. 'OK, you're not doing any work today at all.'

'I have a few more pages of the contract to rea-'

'None. I'm serious. You look a mess, man. Freshen up, get changed out of the clothes you obviously slept in and we'll go out for a proper breakfast and a catch up. No arguments.'

Alastair stares with raised eyebrows for a few seconds, but gives in to Luke's smiling there's-no-point-arguing face with no reluctance whatsoever. He steps towards Luke and they share a hug, clapping each other on the back.

'Thanks so much for coming up. This is so far out of your way, let me at least pay for some petrol.'

'I'll not hear of it, I'm just pleased you weren't in a city further away. You can pay me back by buying a plane ticket for yourself and Nik to come over and see us again next year. We'll have a full guest wing by then, the extension's going great. Now get ready and let's get some food, I'm starving!'

In the time it takes Alastair to shower, Luke tidies all the papers away in page order and puts them in two neat stacks on the coffee table in the lounge part of the suite. He moves the laptop off the bed and opens the rest of the curtains to admire the view. As the bathroom door opens to emit some of the steam that built up Alastair hears him whistle in the other room, impressed by what he sees.

'They really pushed the boat out on this hotel room, huh?' Luke shouts through.

'Yeah, I think it's because I'm here for such a long while. Now that I know why I wish I hadn't come.' He dresses himself gradually as they talk, having taken fresh clothes into the bathroom with him.

'Oh? They back-pedalling?'

'Not exactly, they've just issued a new negotiation pack that's making changes to nearly everything they originally agreed to over email and conference call. They said they wanted me here for so long to learn the inner workings of the business and my work ethic, but seems it was so they could do a one-eighty and drop this new terms pack.'

'Hmmm that's a bit shitty of them, you regretting trying to acquire them?'

'I'm not sure yet, I started to wonder if maybe I should be happy with what I have already. The company does so well back home as it is. I'm not sure why it was decided we would start reaching out overseas. I think the board suggested it.'

'It's your company, you can do what you want. If you're content with what you have then stuff the board. They are one hundred percent just looking for more opportunity to line their pockets, but that's never been your style.'

'Thank you for saying so. I guess you're right.'

'But enough about work. Let's go and get a hearty, cholesterol-building breakfast. You look like you need it even after that shower.'

'Oh, thanks.'

The size of the breakfasts in the diner they choose is phenomenal, and as the plate is presented to him Alastair's unnoticed hunger claws from the back of his mind to the forefront. He meets Luke's eye with as much sincerity as he can before tucking in.

'Thank you. I really needed this. To be pulled out of my slump and have some decent food put in front of me. This week has been ridiculous. I've not been looking after myself properly, I know.'

'You don't need to thank me, it's what friends do. You'd do the same if I was messaging late at night seeming extremely stressed and then stopped replying without warning. I've been there with the stress and I don't wish it on anyone.'

'How are the kids and Melanie doing?'

'They're great, honestly I feel so lucky. I don't regret leaving London, I was pushing myself to an early grave. I don't want you doing the same. The company does great, like you say, and it's a good size to remain manageable. If you're only here on the board's desires I'd suggest going home after this trip and cancelling the merger. So many companies reach out overseas and it becomes the death of them. That's my professional advice to you, and the last I'll say about it. Now to the more important stuff. How's Nik doing? Is she OK home alone?'

Alastair stores Luke's words, filing them away to consider later. 'She seems OK generally, but she's been sounding a little strange the past few days. Like, focused but distant at the same time. Herself but not. I dunno. She struggles with being home alone a lot and I want to believe she can handle it, but I can only go by what I can glean from her over the phone.'

'Is she not honest about how she's doing, is that why you're worried?' Luke spears a sausage with gusto as he asks.

'It's not that she lies, per se, it's just she wants to be doing OK with it so she pretends she is. She also doesn't like to worry me so sometimes she says what I want to hear instead of what she feels, but I've learned to tell the difference now.'

'Seems you both have a habit of not wanting to worry each other, but be careful that doesn't lead to you never speaking your minds to one another. Next time you speak with her, maybe let her know that and give her the chance to be honest, or more direct.'

'It does get a bit exhausting trying to decode and read what she really means.' The advice is as good as the heavenly bacon Alastair just tried. His battery is flat, and the food is recharging it. 'I just wish she didn't feel she has to do that around me.'

'It's because she loves you. I did it for Melanie. I didn't want to see the look on her face when I'd tell her it had been another bad day at the office. Nik doesn't want to keep seeing you look sad when she says she's not feeling well. It sounds like she's come a long way in the last year or so, though?'

'She has. She really has. She's being so strong, and she's getting depressed less often. I hope I've helped at least a little, sometimes I wonder if I make her worse.' The toast is equally fantastic, energy returns to him with every bite. Luke isn't hanging around with his food, he clears two-thirds of his plate in the time Alastair clears one. How can someone eat that fast and manage to avoid talking with their mouth full?

'You don't. Trust me, you don't. You're like Nik in that way, you know?'

'What do you mean?'

'You can't see your own value. I think the only reason she's getting strong enough to fight it off is because of you. Just being there and putting that effort in is more than enough. You make all the difference to her, even if it doesn't feel like it most of the time.' The mouthful of food is hard to swallow as Luke's words fill Alastair's chest. 'I'll tell you for her, as someone who had to tell their partner the same. You do make a difference.' If there's anyone in the world he doesn't mind tearing up in front of, it's Luke. His words push away all his doubts, all his concerns, as though laying bare a truth Alastair can't see himself. Without another word Luke passes him a napkin, smiles and nods. There's no need to say thank you, and Alastair knows it.

'You know, you've made me feel much better than Edward did the other night. I don't remember if you know him?'

'You mentioned you went for a meal with him which didn't go that well, but I didn't want to pry. What happened?' They both take a sip of their coffees at the same time.

'Yeah we met for a catch up and dinner. I accidentally let slip that Nik wasn't well and when I told him why because he seemed concerned he was so dismissive.'

'Dismissive?'

'Long story short he basically told me I should leave Nik and find someone who would make me happier and who wasn't such hard work, because I sounded like her carer.'

'Are you serious? That's disgusting.'

It's validating to hear Luke defend him with the same sentiments he felt towards Edward on the night of the meal. 'I got so mad, I left the restaurant after telling him what I thought about him. I haven't been that angry for a long while.'

'I should think so, he sounds like a complete dick. He's obviously never had to struggle with any mental illnesses a day in his life or have any friends that struggle. If he did I wouldn't be surprised if they kept it a secret from him with an attitude like that. That's actually made me mad.'

'I just couldn't believe his reaction. I suppose not everyone is as informed about it as me or you though.'

'That's true, but when a friend tells you something like that you're meant to support them, not encourage them to bail on their partner. Geez.' Luke sips his coffee with a sassy attitude and Alastair loves him for it. He misses Luke a lot since he moved over here, but he'll definitely get plane tickets for him and Nik next year. 'Well, I've eaten enough to last me the whole weekend. You're putting on a poor show, Al.'

'It's the most amazing breakfast, but I really can't eat

another thing. Two-thirds isn't bad! I think I need to walk it off.'

'Let's take a walk around the city, it's been ages since I've been here.'

The weather is clear but the breeze has a slight chill. It's packed with people, every street full of those heading to their destinations with purpose, either running errands on their only free day, mulling around window shopping, fulfilling all their wants and needs.

They walk and talk and walk some more. No aim other than to enjoy each other's company and not stress about work, or anything. Eventually they tire and Luke suggests they head back to the hotel. When they make it back they slump on the bed, kicking off their shoes and relishing the rest.

'What a day. I feel totally refreshed.' Alastair sighs, sinking into the bed. The fresh air still zips around his lungs.

'I should come over to England more often and drag you out over there too.'

'You should, we'd love to have you.'

'Good to hear. Well, do you think I can get away with bunking in here tonight or will I have to book my own room? If I leave you alone for the rest of the weekend you'll only end up working. It's my man-friend duty to stay and make sure you're thoroughly distracted.'

'You'll stay the whole weekend?'

'You could do with the company, so long as you don't mind?'

'Of course I don't. Sounds like the perfect weekend to

me, and I don't mind blaming you for me not getting my work done.'

'That settles it then, you're stuck with me until the end of tomorrow.' They laugh. Truly laugh.

# SIXTEEN
## Nikkita

*I can't look at them yet. I need one more. One from a stranger. Someone I've never even encountered before, who will see me for the first time and then I can see how I look to them. How can I get them to hold the prism? I can't just hand it to them. "Here will you hold my magic prism while it steals your perception of me?" I'd just seem crazy. I worry enough about that... about seeming crazy. I hope I don't.*

Nik spent the best part of the last week visiting people. Family, the few friends she has, people she hasn't seen since school, people she sees often but not socially like the cashier at the local corner shop and the barista at the cafe she frequents with Ellie. She hasn't told Alastair what's happening. She can't. She fears she'll sound the way she feels: Obsessed.

The prism is never out of reach. If she isn't running her fingers over its smooth surface she's fiddling with it, trying to work out more of its secrets. She's discovered projection mode, and run-on mode, as she calls them. Now she can have the prism show the images without having to lift it to her eye. She makes sure to hold her palm in front of a white or plain surface and watches as the top panels all open, creating a little bubble in which she can view whichever perception she selects. She may have collected a good few, but she hasn't viewed the new ones yet. She wants to wait until she has the view of a total stranger.

She has a small notebook filled with scribbled considerations of who to approach and why. Which set of views will give her the best spread of positive perceptions? If she's going to build up a library of evidence against her own opinion it has to be strong. That's why she's picked people she knows, in the hopes they'll all be good. That negative voice, still itching away with its comments, chirps in but far less often. It feeds her with a string of doubts and possibilities.

*They'll all hate you. Even your parents will think you're ugly. You're collecting evidence to help me, not prove me wrong. You'll see when you sit down to view them.*

*You're wrong. I haven't collected all these, made sure all these people touched the prism, just to prove you right. Keep your nose out of it.*

*I'm hardly going to sit by while you try and get rid of me. You're nothing without me.*

*That's really what you think? I have a feeling I'm more without you.*

*You're not. You've never been alone, never without me. You're scared, I can feel it. Can smell it on you. You don't want to go and get a stranger's view because you can't guarantee what it'll be like. You're foolish enough to think that everyone you've collected so far will be good, but you don't know what to believe of a stranger. The moment you're faced with a reality you don't want you're trying to turn tail and run.*

*It is scary. Why wouldn't it be? Finding out what kind of impression you make on a total stranger.*

*Why do you care what they think?*

*Why don't you?*

There's no answer, but now she's even more determined to go out and find what she's missing. *If I just go out there and find one, then I can view all the others. Go to the supermarket. The one that's a little further away. Find someone there, get them to hold the prism then come straight home. Then you can see them all and you can know for certain.*

She's ready to go. She's been ready for almost an hour. She grasps at a thin tendril of courage, collects her bag, prism safely stored in her most secure pocket, and leaves.

The supermarket isn't all that busy. She's thankful for that as she collects a trolley. There are a few things she needs. It isn't like she came here just for the perception. Perception shopping. It almost makes her laugh, but it isn't enough to cut through her nerves, which jangle like keys. She wanders around the aisles unhurried, taking the items she needs but focusing more on scrutinising the other shoppers. *It doesn't really matter who it is*, she tells herself. *Looking for someone you think is more likely to like you defeats the point of the exercise entirely. The next time you're in an aisle with only one other person, accidentally drop the prism as you pass them. Hopefully they'll pick it up and return it, and if not you can just turn around and retrieve it.*

Each aisle gives her a new excuse not to do it.

*Too many people. The children might pick it up. She looks angry already. What if they steal the prism?*

Eventually she's left in an aisle with a middle-aged-looking man who seems to be of neutral mood as he inspects the back of a soup can.

*OK, just drop it. It's wrapped in a little hanky, it'll be fine, it won't break. Just gently let it drop.*

She gives the prism a final, apologetic squeeze and drops it as she walks past the man. It takes a lot of effort not to turn around and look, to bend down and pick it straight up off of the floor. To polish it with a tissue and apologise. She just keeps walking. One. Slow. Step. At. A. Time.

'Excuse me, is this yours?'

She turns, smiling. 'Sorry?'

'I think you dropped this?' The hanky is still on the floor, the prism must have rolled out of it. She hears the hum that he won't be able to comprehend as it takes the snapshot. Bending to retrieve the hanky she displays her kindest expression.

'Oh, thank you so much! I would hate to lose this. Thank you.'

'No problem.' He turns his attention back to his soup cans with only the slightest twitch of the mouth. He was fascinated by the prism, she saw it in his face as he held it. A pointless worry that he wouldn't give it back battered against her chest, but it's in her hands now. It's captured what it needs to. She continues with her shop, unsure what to feel. She has all the perceptions she wants to collect, the next step is viewing them.

*Do I really want to, though? Is this such a good idea? Isn't Alastair's view enough?*

She contemplates it, trying not to be sad about the fact that she's collected more views because she doesn't trust Alastair's alone. He's biased towards her, he's always thought her beautiful. She needs more than that if she wants to truly believe it. She needs many perspectives, yet she's contradicted herself in only collecting views from people she knows until this one. It's scary to consider getting views from strangers. Maybe she needs more. Could she add another two or three strangers to balance it out? To make things fairer? Her thoughts turn to Alastair. Today or tomorrow they're due to have their little call. Catch up on the events they've experienced, or lack of them. *What would he say if he knew what I've been doing?*

The gift was meant to help her, not cause anxiety. He'd probably be angry that she's even concerned with what strangers think of her. He'd fly off the handle a bit, if only out of love. He's done it regarding Emma before and that's someone she knows. When it comes to the fact she's an inherent people-pleaser he's even more strict.

"You can't keep catering to everyone, Nik. It's OK to do things for yourself, you know? It's OK not to want to do something or go somewhere for someone else. You need to learn to be a bit selfish instead of always going out of your way for others, especially when it doesn't do you any good. I know you hate conflict, and you hate disappointing people, but you're a doormat and I don't like it. You deserve better."

It's not to say Alastair doesn't help people, or doesn't want her helping people. Quite the opposite. He's one of the kindest people she knows, and he encourages others to help people where they can but not to the point of self-detriment.

There has to be a line, he often says, a point at which you consider whether you really are too tired to go out and give someone a lift home. Too busy to look over peoples' documents for free or as a favour, which has been common among her friends or family because she's editorially inclined. He always says how she's been working all day already and should tell them they'll have to wait a few days. She never can, though, she does things as soon as she receives them. She's never unavailable to help, even when she doesn't want to, even when it's wholly inconvenient or costly to her. It drives Alastair mad. She's trying, though. Trying to be more selective with what she does and doesn't help with. She doesn't want to be a doormat, but it disappoints people when she refuses things, which in turn makes her feel very guilty.

The train of thought leads her all the way through the shop, and her trolley is full of things she needs but doesn't remember putting in there. It's time to head home. Time to see the truth once and for all. Alastair may not believe it matters what others think, but it matters to Nik. She seeks value from others because she believes she has none and will never find it without their help. She's doing what she wants, just like Alastair so often suggests. She's helping herself, and she's ready to see what that'll get her.

# SEVENTEEN
## Nikkita

The notebook and the prism shake in her hands and she makes her way to the sofa. The same sofa where she figured out all the secrets of the prism. Where she cried after Emma brought out the selfish part of her. Where she sits on the days she can't bring herself to work because she doesn't want to fail and go to bed. It seems odd to her that so much could have happened in this one spot. Does the sofa cushion take it all in? Storing it to wrap around her the next time she sits on it? Maybe emotions leave behind a fingerprint too, forever staining the places we sit when we feel things and the clothes we wear when we let it all go. She can never wash herself clean. Depression cakes her in a grime. Dirty and so clogged that emotions don't register. What she wouldn't give to feel the opposite. To be washed clean of all the negative, to allow space for the positive to take root. She pins all her hopes for this on the prism and what it might show her in the next few minutes.

The perceptions are ordered, she saw to that by collecting them in the order she wants to see them. It can be changed, if you know how, just like she figured out the projection mode. There's one more thing she discovered in her endless fiddling and what felt like decryption. She isn't allowed to look at the prism more than once an hour, but that doesn't mean she can only view one perception per hour. There's a way to make the prism cycle through everything it has collected so far one after the other. That's how the plan formed in her mind, the plan to gather all these views and then play them one by one. She can see each of them every hour if she wants. The main infuriating thing is that there's still no way to remove gathered perceptions as far as she can tell. She longs to be rid of Emma's. Anger flares in her every time she thinks of it, but now isn't the time for that. Now is the time for calm and open minds.

    She runs through each person on the list. She has Alastair, Emma and Ellie already, then she collected both parents, a friend she hasn't seen since high school, the till attendant at their local corner shop, the barista at the cafe, a neighbour, and the stranger from the supermarket. It's a good spread, but it was decidedly awkward to contact the old friend. Neither party had all that much interest in the other's lives, and neither of them would bother making contact again. She passed it off as making efforts to get back in touch, but their differences were clear. She used the old 'drop the prism on her way out' trick just like at the supermarket. It's time to stop reminiscing and just do it.

    'I want to see but I don't. What if they do all think I'm ugly? What if I hear awful thoughts they've had about me? Will I even recognise myself through their eyes? How am I supposed to handle this alone?'

    *Well who else will do it for you? You've yelled at me that things are going to change from now on, but you seem no different to me. Not strong enough to take anything on your own back, happy to sit by and let others do everything for you.*

'That's not true! I went out and collected everything didn't I? I did that for myself, no one else.'

*Did you? I thought you were doing that for Alastair? So you could feel happy for him, show him you're more than the miserable git he has to look after.*

'He doesn't see me that way, I know that now. Stop your poisonous spouting and let me get on with this.' The malice in her own thoughts surprises her, but she doesn't regret it. There's no reply. The prism looks so ornamental on the small table in front of her. The carpet beneath it is a light beige, so it will be easy to see the projections as there are no patterns to interfere with them. Once more she ensures that everything is set up properly, that she's programmed the prism correctly. Her heartbeat thuds in her ears, one leg bounces up and down as she twists the prism in the correct direction and waits.

They fade in and disappear one after the other. A Nikkita parade. Each different than the last in ways so subtle they are hard to distinguish. Yet they're still so clearly individual. Some pretty, some plain, some happy, sad, grumpy and some... ugly. No two are the same, and the whispers of each perception flutter around her ears. With each new version she recognises her true self less and less. Drifting further and further away from her internal anchor. It's like a group of artists each trying to draw her in their own personal style.

Her mother thinks her beautiful and is reluctantly

proud of her, her father not so much. He wanted a boy, or so the prism told her, and did all he could to see her in that light. Neither approve of her career choice. She never would have known. Never suspected. The old friend finds her tiresome, a goody-two-shoes even now, and not a pretty one. The till attendant thinks she needs to comb her hair more, but doesn't find her unattractive. The girl at the coffee shop thinks she's gorgeous, and Nik blushes. She never expected to have an admirer.

The last though, is reminiscent of how Emma sees her. The stranger. That one is ugly, grumpy and scowling. It erases all the ones before it. Skittling them with a bowling ball of disbelief.

'I haven't even met him before. How can he think so little of me? I wasn't rude, I smiled at him, I thanked him. I was this ugly to a total stranger?'

*Do you see now? The truest perception, the most unbiased, is the one of the stranger. When people meet you that's what they see. A miserable, ugly, disgusting thing.*

'How can he judge me like that? How can he be that way to someone he doesn't know? It's horrible. He just stood there with his stupid, crooked glasses reading the back of soup cans. Who even does that? Casting judgement on all those around him as they pass him by? He must be a sad, miserable man himself to be doing such a thing. Judging people like that is wrong. He doesn't even know me.'

*And what are you doing right now?*

Nik's skin turns cold at the allegation as it blooms in her mind. 'What?'

*Isn't that what you're doing to him right this second? Judging without knowing him?*

'I...' She is. She's doing just what she berated him for. The realisation closes in on her, and then draws her breath away. 'I thought I was a good person, I try to be. I was polite to him, I do everything I can for everyone else, and this is still how I'm seen? I'm... I'm judgmental too. Good people aren't like that, they don't judge like that.'

*Well, we know what that means don't we? You're not a good person like you thought. You're as bad as that stranger. Seeing the negative in people first.*

'No. I always look for the good in people. I put up with Emma for years even though I knew she was using me.'

*But you were angry about it. You didn't want to listen to her drone on about her non-problems. You were two-faced. You always have been. Sitting and listening to her, agreeing with her, when all you wanted to do was tell her to get a grip and that her problems weren't real. Are you saying you never thought those things while you sat across from her pretending to care?*

'I did care! I just... wish she cared about me too. What about me? Why should I get walked all over, I have my own stuff to deal with.'

*But you don't deal with it, you ignore it, let it take over you. You lie in bed, useless and lazy and let it take its course.*

'I can't, OK? I can't always do it. It's OK not to be OK sometimes.'

*Emma wasn't OK. Maybe that stranger wasn't OK either. Maybe he was lonely, maybe he saw the quizzical look you were throwing at him while he stood reading his soup, and maybe that's why he disliked you. You were judging him before he even did you that kindness of picking up the prism. He could have ignored it because of how you looked at him.*

'I... I didn't mean...' All those artists trying to draw her, they elbow each other with vicious nudges, all fighting to paint the same canvas. The image of herself is smeared, muddled, unrecognisable. 'You're right. I never thought I was like that. That kind of person. I judged him, decided he was weird and strange, yet I asked his help. Why? Why am I like this? If I am, then why does he love me? Why does Alastair love me at all? I don't understand. He's so kind and thoughtful, he shouldn't be with someone like me, someone who's unkind and unfeeling.'

Her mind spirals out of her control. Bad thought after bad thought seems more reasonable, more convincing. The evidence is tipping in their favour. It's easier to believe the bad in people. In herself. Everyone does, don't they? All the perceptions she collected, most of them are more beautiful than she thinks herself, but the bad ones are the ones she clings to. A sail in a harsh wind of negativity, dragging her around in a sea of conflict and confusion. Why does the opinion of a stranger matter more than those of her closest family and friends?

'It doesn't. It doesn't matter more. There were so many versions, why can't I focus on the good ones.'

*You can't just bury the bad ones and hope they aren't true. You'd choose to take the good over the bad just to make yourself feel better?*

'But... my family and friends and Alastair all know me. Doesn't that make their perceptions a more accurate reflection? I have to see. I have to see Alastair's again. He knows me better than anyone, his is the truth.'

*You're lying to yourself.*

'I'm not, you're trying to make me do that.'

*Go ahead and look. Even though you only just saw. Break the rules.*

'The rules... I can't. I can't look for another forty-five minutes.'

*You need to. You have to look, so you can see how his perception has changed.*

'Changed?'

*You don't think it would? Now you've admitted the truth about yourself you still think he'd see you the same way?*

'It hasn't changed. It wouldn't change.'

*Then check.*

'I can't.'

*You need to. There's no other way to know. The rules don't matter. You keep saying how you're stronger now, how you can fight me now, then prove me wrong. Show me he still thinks you're pretty.*

A pressure sinks into her lungs. She needs him here. Needs him to tell her she isn't a bad person as well as ugly. She can see part of him if she looks at the prism. She shouldn't. She's never broken the rules before. Never looks when she hates or feels negative about herself, never looks more than once an hour.

'The prism won't punish me. We're connected now. It shared all its secrets with me.' Her hand is reaching for it before she consciously makes the decision. 'Just this once. I'll only break the rules once, I really need to see. I need proof that I'm not ugly. That I'm not a horrible person. I can't call it truth without seeing it, I can't fight it alone.'

She turns the prism once clockwise and raises it to her

eye. There she is. Stunning. Sun-kissed. With her flowing hair and genuine smile. Alastair's loving thoughts envelop her, but then... the edges of the image turn black. Tendrils of dark smoke wrap around her smiling self, strangling her, scorching her skin. Changing her into the only self she's ever recognised. The ugly one.

'No... NO. Stop it! No don't erase it DON'T take it away please. DON'T TAKE IT FROM ME!'

# EIGHTEEN
## Nikkita

Intermittent sobs burst from Nik as she fumbles with the prism in desperation, executing every turn and tap hoping to stop whatever trail of destruction she's started. Nausea rises and works alongside the black smoke to push her to the edge of hysteria. Tears cloud her eyes and she stands facing an abyss of hopelessness as the creeping vapour changes the scene she's come to love. All that's reflected in the prism now is her own perception. It's ugly, disgusting. But what of the others? Flicking through one by one her panic rises to a fever pitch. They're all changing, transforming, she's losing them all, losing everything. Her mind tumbles and stirs, her heart twists and contorts in great turns.

'It can't be gone, they can't all be gone. Please just give Alastair's back, just that one, I need it. I just had to see. I wanted to feel better, isn't that what you were for?' Her taps and turns are useless, all colour drains from the prism's marbled surface. Nik slumps, resigning to her failure, and the prism sits in her palm with its lustre stripped away. Is it broken? Will it ever work again? Her sobs and sniffs fill the silent corner of the house, it's all she can do not to wail in regret. In grief. In anger.

'Why did I look? Why did I fucking look? I knew the rules, I just had to see, I needed his perception. Is it so bad just to do it once? I worked hard for the prism, unlocking all its secrets. It was one time. Once. Stupid thing betrayed me for breaking the rules once. I thought we were connected, I thought it trusted me. I gave it everything, all my attention, I did what it wanted didn't I? Why couldn't you just show me that one extra time?'

She isn't aware she's speaking to the prism. She isn't aware of all that much just now. 'I thought you understood me. You betrayed me. Why did you take it? The only thing I had. Why did you change it?' She raises her arm to throw the prism across the room, a motion filled with certainty for all of a few seconds before she crumples into renewed, shaking sobs and holds it close. She can't dispose of it. They can figure it out together, can't they? They have to be able to repair what she's done.

'I'm sorry... I'm so sorry. I knew the rules and I broke them anyway. I just felt so ugly, so worthless right then that I needed proof it wasn't true, that's all it was. I'm sorry for what I did.' Her hands turn clammy. Sweat. Or is it? She opens her palm and her face contorts in disgust. Thick, black liquid seeps and oozes from the surface of the prism's panels. It starts to sizzle, burning her hands. In recoil she throws it on to the carpet where it skitters before coming to rest in a pool of the strange treacle. The liquid turns to vapour, a liquorice-black, slow-moving cloud that creeps like lava across her floor... towards her.

The sofa-back stops her retreat, she only pushes herself further into the cushions, trapping herself. They feel as though they might swallow her. *Move. Move! You have to move!* Scrambling sideways she lollops onto the floor, bare feet scraping around as she searches for the energy to push herself forward. The smoke continues its lethargic advance and tendrils test the air like snake tongues. She sees the moment they catch her scent or presence and the flow changes direction. It's impossible to look away, the folds of the fog smear across her floor. Her arms work in a pathetic backstroke, dragging her away a few inches at a time as her feet flail about, nails pulling strands of carpet free.

It spills faster now, matching her speed, hunting her. With a yelp and a crack of pain her spine comes against the leg of the oak dining table and a desperate whimper escapes her. *Get up. Get up and run. You have to. GET UP!* Manoeuvring into a clumsy crouch Nik grabs the lip of the table and pulls herself up, still unable to tear her eyes off of the advancing smoke she retreats backwards. Her hip stings as it collides with the corner of the cabinet in the hallway. Feet sticking to the laminate. She has to get upstairs, she doesn't know why. It isn't as if the smoke can't climb them.

The ceiling swings to the front of her vision in an unexpected swoop. The damned rug. She tripped on it. Winded, crying, drained of energy. The smoke rounds the corner into her hallway like a victorious vapour serpent. It moves easier on the laminate. Her eyes widen in horror as it swallows her legs, damp and without warmth. It has a grip, but why does it need one? Then she begins to slide across the floor. Her nails scrape against anything she can reach, door frames, the cabinet edge, the table legs, the corner of the sofa. She passes each landmark again in reverse. Choking out sobs and struggling with renewed fervour. Her energy has come too late.

'No don't, don't take me in there, I don't want to go in. Let me go let me go let me GO.' As the prism claims her a disorienting feeling washes forward. A digital blaring drifts through water. The phone. The phone is ringing. Alastair. It must be Alastair. 'Al help me! Let me get to him. No. No stop let me go let me get to the phone ALASTAIR!'

The world grows. Or does she shrink? It's impossible to tell. As the black smoke covers her in its deadly blanket her pleas become inane and surpass even her own understanding. She's just been dragged across the floor of her own home by the prism. She belongs to it now. She can feel its claim on her. Its wrath. She broke the rules. She deserves it. It will trap her. Imprison her. It takes her perceptions from her, and now it takes her. The world turns black like the smoke that smothered her, and the distorted ringing of the phone cries in the distance like a lost child. All that's left in her living room is the lingering echo of her shouts and the prism sitting innocently enough on the carpet, its outer panels twinkling with marbled black and grey.

# NINETEEN
## Nikkita

Nik's eyes are too heavy to open, and part of her doesn't want to look. Concentrating on what she knows for sure makes her feel a bit more focused.

*I'm face-down. Lying on some sort of grass. It's sharp, dry. Feels dead. I'm outside? There's wind. There are whispers travelling on it. Don't listen. It's not cold. The wind has no temperature. There's no other sound. The grass doesn't smell of anything. There's a lot of space around me. I feel so small. I don't want to see, but I have to look. Just sit up first. Do what you do when you're depressed, what Alastair taught you to do. One small thing at a time.*

Rolling over. That's step one. Just rolling over. It's a great effort. Her body is made of lead, stiffness fighting every movement. Breathing comes easier on her back, and the light beyond her lids becomes bright, intrusive.

At least that means there's probably a sky. A sun? A few deep breaths calm her racing heart.

*OK, so, I'm outside... somewhere. I'm oriented. It looks bright out here. I'll take my time.*

Her face doesn't feel any different. Hadn't the prism warped her appearance as punishment, turned her into some kind of ugly creature for not valuing herself? Seems not. At least not yet.

She resigns herself to the fact that the most likely place she could be… is inside the prism.

A shudder bolts through her as she remembers being dragged through her home.

*OK, so I'm in the prism. I deserve it. God how stupid could I be? I knew the rules. I thought I was above them. I have to figure out how to get back. If Alastair was calling and I don't pick up he'll get worried. You got yourself into this mess. Time to do something about it. Slowly open your eyes and find out where you are.*

She has to shield her eyes to open them. Whatever is above her is bright, achingly so. Pure white, unspoiled by any other colours or marks of any kind. Once adjusted she takes in her surroundings. There isn't much to see, but at the same time too much. Nik is sitting in the expanse of a vast black-grassed plain. Nothing grows, the grass is scorched and dry as tinder. In the distance it meets with a sky of clinically clean white, as though any colour it once possessed has been drained away by constant bleaching. It's oddly beautiful. The simplicity of the dark and the light, and the silence, the stillness of the air around her.

The plain isn't entirely flat, and Nik has visions of creatures lurking behind the hillocks or in the dips. Doing a full turn, staring in awe, she spots a shimmer in the distance. It isn't much, but it's a direction to walk in for now. Anything is better than standing still in the emptiness that surrounds her. She feels as though she's wearing a big target on her back. Walking is safer than being still, or so she tells herself. She pulls herself up onto hollow, shaky legs and begins moving one step at a time.

After what could have been either a few minutes or half an hour the shimmer in the distance appears closer.

Hoping it's true, she pushes away the concern that it's a mirage like the ones people lost in the desert often mistake for water. There's been a suspicious lack of activity from her negative voice. Is that why she feels so determined? So willing to forge on? Where's the tirade of laughter, accusations and insults? Surely it should be revelling in her predicament, but there isn't so much as a whisper to needle her. With a fool's grin she sees that the shimmer isn't a mirage. There are rocks, and a boulder or two, in a ring around the sparkling surface. The grass turns to black sand a few steps ahead. There are two figures. People! They must be able to help her. A deep-rooted thirst shoves her caution aside. Water. Water and people. There might be hope after all, but stay cautious. Don't be reckless.

The crisp crunch of the blackened ground beneath her unsure feet becomes rhythmic, it could go on forever, ticking like a forgotten but reliable clock. Left, right, left, right. Nerves flutter as the two figures around the pond, as she can now see that's the source of the glimmering, come into clearer view. They flutter more with each step until they tremble, the instant the nerves turn to fear her legs become sluggish. The sand turns to treacle. She recognises one of them. That's why her mind has been left undisturbed. She's here.

Nik can't stop her own advance, the hypnotising tick-tock of her gait is now beyond her control. The two figures turn to face her. Ten steps to the edge of the pond. *That's me.* Nine. *So is that one.* Eight. *They're both me.* Seven. *I'm me, too.* Six. *We're all me.* Five. *I know that one.*

Four. *She's... the me I see.* Three. *The other one... that's Alastair's version of me, or Ellie's?* Two. *What's going on?* One. *Why are they staring?*

'I knew you'd screw it up.' Her ugly self laughs maliciously. It's more ugly than Nik remembers. More... feral. 'Always thinking only of yourself, now here you are.'

'Quiet, Nothing. Being nasty won't help. She must be terrified not having a clue where she is.'

The other reflection of her is so pretty that Nik can barely reconcile with the fact that it's her. Her smile is kind and compassionate, brow creased with concern. Her hair is bright and beams with blonde vitality despite there being no sun to light it. Her figure is one Nik only dreams of having. 'You must be quite confused, yes?' Nik nods.

'Serves her right.'

'Shush, you bated her into it.'

'She was saying she was strong enough to do without me. Obviously she was lying.'

'You're just as dependent on her as she is on you.'

'I don't need her, why would I? Look at her, she's not worth needing.' As the argument continues, and she watches herselves argue with one another, anxiety batters the inside of her chest.

*Stop.*

The biting words crowd together, hanging in the air, colliding with each other.

'That's enough, how can you say such a thing about her. She's come all the way here.'

'Not by choice. She was dragged here for being a defiant bitch and breaking the rules of the prism.'

*Stop.*

The malice sparks off of the empathy, filling the space around them with a fog of confusion. It presses in around Nik, smearing itself all over her. Clammy against her skin, raising goosebumps in the thick sludge of conflict.

'She just needed to see me. She needed to feel loved and pretty, you can't blame her for that. You can't blame anyone for that. You're the one who pushed her. It's because of you that she needed me.'

'She'll still choose me.'

*Stop it.*

The water ripples still. It doesn't look like normal water. It's thick but crystal clear. Nik can't see the bottom, but wonders if that's the thing calling to her. If nothing else, it's clear she can't use it to comfort her scratchy throat.

'Why would anyone choose you? You offer nothing but hatred and malice. Why won't you let anyone in to help you? You haven't even opened up to me.'

'Why would I open up to you? You're a lie. A fabrication placed by him to trick her into thinking she's nicer than she is. More beautiful. He's only doing it for himself.' Her voices layer and echo, writhing in muffled combat. Nik's chest begins to tighten and constrict.

'Alastair cares about Nik more than you'll ever know!' Their voices rise, more accusatory with every exchange. It's like Nik isn't even there.

*Maybe I'm not here. Maybe I never was.*

The stillness of the water hums to her. A hum she wishes was louder. A hum to drown out the arguing.

*Maybe these two can manage without me. The water is so still. I wish I was that still. Could this be the water that can wash me clean?*

'She has to choose one of us. You know how it works. Why would she choose you, a stranger, an imposter and a fake?'

'Because I'm new. I'm not like you. I'd take care of her, help her realise her worth, not chip away at it for fun and games.'

'And who would want that? Who would want to strut around believing they had such worth? It's arrogant, self-important, self-serving.'

'We all have to serve ourselves sometimes. You're doing it by continuing to tread her down.'

'STOP IT!' Nik had no intent to shout out loud. Both her reflections bite back their retorts. Nik doesn't take her eyes off of the surface of the water. 'What do you mean I have to choose one of you?' There's an edge to her voice that she hopes isn't too sharp, but she needs to take control of the conversation before her mind splits into three.

'That's why you're here, stupid. When you broke the rules you were brought to the prism plains, but you can't leave unless you make a decision. Which one of us do you want to be?' Nothing grins with spite.

'Which do I want to be?'

'Whoever you choose will become your reflection on the outside. You don't get to keep your original appearance. You never acknowledged it anyway so you won't miss it.'

'You aren't my true reflection?'

'As much as you believed it, no, I'm not. But you need me. You'll choose me. I've been here all along. Helping you, protecting you, from thoughtless notions like princess prim over there. She'd have you prancing around telling the world how pretty you are. She'd make you arrogant and self-important, but that's not what you want, is it? You want to be humble, you'd rather not believe it than act that way. I'm the one that helped you do that, I'm the one who keeps you grounded.'

'That's not what I'd do, Nik. I wouldn't make you into that kind of person. I would help you love yourself. I'd help you to see how beautiful you really are, inside and out, how kind and caring. I'd help you to believe it so that you can be happy, so you can see the truth. Look. Look into the reflection of the pond and see. It will show your true face, your true self. But do not touch it. Do not disturb the water.'

Which was telling the truth? Were either of them? How can she know, how can she trust? She leans out over the pond, feeling its odd resonance more prominently. Her reflection ripples into view and she gasps.

It's not as pretty as the self that Alastair sees, but it's nowhere near as ugly and out of shape as Nothing. It's pretty in a natural way. The way Ellie sees her is the closest perception she's seen to the one that stares back at her with teary eyes in the unusual liquid.

'This is me? But.. I'm not ugly at all here. And now I can't go back this way? I have to pick one or the other? That's not fair! Why should I lose something I didn't know I had, something I've only just found?'

'Because you never appreciated it. You never wanted to acknowledge it. You don't deserve it.'

'She does! She deserves the chance to recognise it. She'll never choose you, you've done nothing but damage her, damage that I haven't even begun to undo.'

'You'll fail. She has to want to change for your tricks to work. She doesn't. She never will. I won't let her.'

They continue to bicker with increasing viciousness. Nik can only cry, a tear falling as a sob jolts her body. She falls to her knees and watches as the ripples from her tear spread across the pond. They lap against both edges. If only the ripple had gone one way, if only it gave her the answer. Though maybe... there's another option.

With a deep breath she sends her love to Alastair on a whisper of the heart, and without a word she lets go. Lets herself plunge into the thick liquid of the pond.

It consumes her, and for the first time in her life she feels the cleansing freshness of a still mind.

# TWENTY
## Alastair

*She's alright. She's fine. She's probably just busy, could be working in the office and her phone be charging downstairs or in the bedroom. She could be asleep, she could be out with friends. There are plenty of reasons why she might not have seen your call or be ready to call you back. She's been sounding odd lately but nothing concerning. Nothing... disturbing.*

Alastair paces the hotel suite, finding the longest route he can before turning around and walking back the other way. It's more like doing laps really.

The phone lies on the bed, turned up to full volume, and he's ready to jump for it the second it rings. Every time he passes it on his small lap of the room he picks it up and taps the screen twice, looking for notifications that Nik has called back.

Nothing.

He's tried several times, increasingly so after a couple of hours passed by with no reply. Two sides of his brain vie for dominance. The reasonable one, and its unfavourable opposite.

*But she always answers within a few rings. She always has her phone with her, and if she missed your call she phones back within minutes. Something must have happened. What if she got really depressed. So depressed she didn't want to deal with it anymore?*

*Don't even go there, no, she's fine. She'd never do something like that, don't even entertain the idea. Someone would have called me to let me know.*

*What if no one's found her yet?*

*There's nothing to find. I'm not even going to entertain that thought. She's just busy, or asleep, or in the bath, or something else.*

He knows he's being unreasonable. Nik wouldn't ever hurt herself. Her depression has never shown any signs of pushing her in that direction, but now his mind has given him the idea. His lungs stutter with each breath as image after heart-breaking image flashes across his mind for a few seconds at a time. Stuff he doesn't want to see. Stuff he shakes away as quickly as possible.

*There must be someone nearby, someone I can contact to ask them to check on her, to put my mind at rest. No. No I'm sure there's no need, that would be overkill. It's only been two hours and forty-five minutes, that's nothing to worry about. She'll call you back when she's ready and there will be a perfectly reasonable explanation for it.*

The phone is in his hand again, he can't walk past it without picking it up. It's easier and more comforting to hold it. Each minute that passes without a call back ticks like a number on a bomb timer. One tick closer to explosion. The room spins with his concern and he perches on the edge of the bed.

'Please Nik, call me back. Just stop what you're doing, pick up the phone, and call back. Even a message. I know it's stupid but I have to know you're OK.' He desperately wants to call Luke, to share his worries with him, but he doesn't want to be in a call if his phone rings. If it rings.

Why wouldn't it? Eventually she'll call back... won't she? The images flash before him again and tears fill his eyes. 'She wouldn't do that. She would never do anything like that. Please stop.' But his mind won't stop. No matter how hard he tries, and his grief at the mere thought of the more sinister reasons why Nik won't answer the phone smothers him like an Alastair-sized plastic bag. With each passing minute his phone stays quiet, more and more air is sucked from the barrier of worry that surrounds him.

There were days before now where Nik had been so depressed that she was practically non-responsive. She wouldn't eat, barely drank, days where her eyes were open but saw nothing. Nothing he did on those days made any difference that he could see, and those are the times he feels the most useless. What if that's happening now? What if she's lying there in bed alone, not eating, not looking after herself or even moving for days, with no one to care for her?

'I can't let her go through that alone.' He resumes the frantic scrolling through his contact list, but every person he considers he knows to be unavailable or they don't keep in touch with anymore. He can't very well call someone he hasn't spoken to in years and ask them to pop around to his home address to make sure Nik is alright. He reaches the bottom, nothing. Their parents all live too far away, he doesn't have Nik's friends' numbers, but even if he did he wouldn't call Emma, knowing of their recent fracas, and he's never had Ellie's number. Maybe he can find it online? But that would be creepy and inappropriate. He doesn't want to seem like a stalker.

A rolling tangle rises in his chest and he throws the phone against the plush bedding, pushing his empty palms against his damp eyes. 'I can't do anything, again! I don't make the slightest bit of difference. I'm not even there to help her, she could be in pain, really depressed all because I came out here to do business. I left her alone. I can't help her when I'm there and even less when I'm here. Why isn't there anything I can do for her? What good am I if I can't make her feel better? Maybe I should go home? What if she's fine, though? What If I'm just over-tired and over-worried? Please Nik. Please just call me back, whatever you're doing.'

A strange feeling overtakes him. Like someone has gently, and with the greatest of care, scooped out part of his soul and drowned it in thick, still water. He stands stock still, his breath retained, and sees an image of Nik floating under water, with a peaceful and serene expression across her pallid-looking face.

# TWENTY-ONE
## *Nikkita*

It's bliss. Pure, undisturbed bliss. No voices vying for attention, no worries or doubts or niggling feelings of hate. In the suspended quiet Nik's mind opens up, her narrow self-perceptions broaden in part by each view she's seen in the prism to reshape the image she has of herself. Each teaches her a new thing, and they all meld to form truths she never thought she'd know.

It all knits and knots together like an intricate blanket, the strands finding their rightful partners and marrying themselves to allow others to do the same. Patterns of hope and happiness, hard truths and home truths, all come together and cast themselves as a net across her tired mind. It drags away the filth and clots of negativity that have embedded themselves year after year, comment after comment. They're pulled away like plaque on brush bristles. Her mind has never felt clearer than at this moment. This is a place where she can be happy.

There's a ruckus above her, muffled shouts and lethargic splashing. She couldn't care less. She just wants to be embraced further by this peace. It isn't to be. Two hands grip her arms. One gentle, the other rougher and of sharper nail. She's hoisted away, being pulled back through the liquid in a slow and reluctant way. It sticks to her, longing to hold her close and drag her further into the black depths below. She won't surrender the contentment she's found, she'll cling to it and take it with her to the surface. A surface that meets her with a crude dryness and bright, sunless sky. Distorted voices drift into her aural focus, sharpening with each word, puncturing her calm bubble.

'-ere you thinking? Nik? Are you alright? Nik!'

'Maybe she's dying.'

'Oh stop it, Nothing, the pond is dangerous but it wouldn't kill.'

'It has done before.'

'That was their choice. She's coming round. Nik, are you alright?'

'I'm OK. I'm alright.' Something new burns quietly within her. A warm stone radiating with a soft glow from her core. A strength she's never known and is scared to take from, yet it can only be for her and her alone.

'Oh, thank god. Why did you do that? You could have been hurt, or not made it out.'

'I just wanted some quiet. The two of you were arguing. I didn't want to hear it anymore, I've heard it in my head enough. The water was so still… so calm.' The urge to return to the pond rags on her like a dog on a chew toy, but she pushes it away.

'We're sorry, aren't we Nothing?'

'Yes.' It's a curt apology, edged with sulking but also shock. When Nik sits up an odd thought strikes. Her clothes aren't wet. Nor is her hair. Breathing was no trouble while under the pond's surface… maybe she hadn't needed to.

'How did I ... get out? Who pulled me up?'

'We both did.'

'Both of you?' Nothing nods. 'That's what I was hoping.' They both stare at her, incredulous.

'You did that on purpose? Why?' Her pretty self seems genuinely upset at the notion, the concern on her face plain to see.

'Like I said, I needed quiet, and I needed to see what you'd both do. It was to help me make my choice.'

'You've... made a decision?' Nothing smirks, confident it will be her.

'I realised something while I was in there. I feel... different now. Like my mind has been washed clean. I've never felt this clear, this... confident. I know now how I have to see things. There were so many differences in all the perceptions I saw in the prism. No two were the same. If every single one is different, if every person has a new and varied view of me, then worrying about it at all is... pointless. It's a total waste of time. Especially being concerned with those who don't know me.

'First impressions aren't the only ones you can make. All the perceptions of me that were good were from people who've known me for years mostly. That means I mean more than my appearance because that hasn't changed. Perceptions come from our inside selves as well. If I can't control the perceptions of others, I can at least control my own.'

'So, which of us did you choose? Just tell us already, enough with the chatter.' Nothing is impatient, but the other Nik smiles and nods.

'You both worked together to pull me out of the pond, and I need you to work together for me again. I need both of you. Nothing, I need you to keep me in check, to protect me and stop me from getting too lofty. I don't want to become an arrogant and selfish person, but you can help me learn when to say no to others, and when to think about what I want. To stay grounded and be critical when necessary.

'I need you, Alastair and Ellie's view, to lift me up, to help me believe I'm not ugly or nasty, or two-faced or any of that. I need you to agree, to help me see what I've always struggled to see. To help me truly feel beautiful, the way I do right this second. To be happy with who I am and how I look. I can't do this without you, or without Nothing. You're both important, you're both essential. Will you work together to keep me balanced, please?'

The two perceptions size each other up. They glance back at the pond, recalling the panic they felt in tandem when she plunged into the depths which they struggled to retrieve her from.

They'd bickered, blaming the other for her choice to fall into the water, but they'd put that aside with haste and bonded their thoughts, both agreeing they had to work as a team.

Most choose only one or the other, or neither. Some wander the plains, taken by the black grass. Some are swallowed by the pond, thinking it a method of escape, and are taken to its irrevocable abyss by its resonant call. Very few make this choice. The right choice. Nothing smiles, though it's still more of a smirk. Alastair's view beams and reaches out to Nothing, speaking on their behalf.

'Well done, Nik. You made the right decision. I'm sure I can figure out a way to put up with this one. She might be rude and a little violent at times, but I've no doubt there are other qualities to be found. Maybe I'll even manage to get her to brush her hair.'

'You must be kidding?' For a moment both Nik and her pretty self think Nothing will refuse. 'I'll never brush my hair, it'll ruin my menacing look.' Nik sees the first genuine smile from the apparition. 'I suppose I can learn to tolerate you, but you stay on your own side of the pond. I don't need your incessantly cheerful face to be the first thing I see every damn morning.'

Nik is helped to her feet, each perception extending a hand. For a brief moment they are all connected. Each of them smile, but none of them see their three reflections become one on the surface of the water. A tugging sensation radiates from Nik's navel, out through her back.

'It's time to go home, Nik. You're one of the few to choose right. Always remember that. We will look after you from now on. Remember that you're a beautiful person.'

'But not too beautiful, maybe just pretty... in the right light.'

'Thank you both.'

Nik is dragged backwards, her heels scraping through the scorched grass and sand. Tears well up in her eyes, a relief and contentment that's an entirely new sensation. A sense of completeness, but also apprehension. It won't be so simple as an overnight change. She'll have to work together with herself to hold on to what she's found… but now determination burns bright. Now she's more herself than ever, and a flicker of discovery shines in the distance as all else fades to black and the pond and its residents drift away.

# TWENTY-TWO
## Nikkita

The carpet warms beneath her cheek, but lying on the living room floor feels wonderfully cool. It's welcome to feel anything after the barren dryness of the... prism plains?

Most would wonder if it had been a dream, but Nik knows it happened. The same free-minded feeling has followed her home, and she's looking at the world with new eyes. As her vision focuses she sees the prism, just out of reach of her extended arm, and a smile dances across her lips.

Taking things slow she graduates to a kneeling position, reaching forward to the small item and steadying herself on the coffee table as reality tilts left and right. The prism has a new colour. All of them. With white as its base the surface shines in iridescence. It's even more beautiful than before. The way it catches the sun fills her with happiness. Genuine, real, happiness. How long has it been?

Standing is a testing task, one that requires her to take a seat on the sofa first for a few minutes. She knows her first move, the phone. The phone was ringing when she was taken. Her waking mind takes a few extra seconds to push her into action. *Alastair! He'll be worried sick.* Prism safely on the coffee table she fumbles with her phone.

*Twelve missed calls! Has something happened to him?* Then she sees the time. It's early evening... but... the prism took her mid-afternoon. She's been gone for hours? She couldn't have been in there longer than thirty minutes. She had to call him right now.

The phone barely makes it through one call tone.

'Nik? Nik! You're alright? Oh thank god.'

His voice is frantic enough to set her heart racing. 'Al, Al calm down, I'm really sorry. I fell asleep upstairs and my phone was charging down here, it was on vibrate.'

'Are you OK?'

'I'm OK. I'm… great, actually.'

He hesitates. Probably wondering if he heard her correctly. 'You sound... different.'

'I feel different.' She stands, collects the prism and slowly makes her way across the room.

'When you said you'd been taking a nap I thought you must be having a bad day.'

'No, I was just really tired I think.'

'You're really OK?'

'Yeah, were you that worried?' She lifts her foot to the first of the stairs, smiling as she treasures hearing his voice.

'Yeah, I guess... I guess because you didn't answer for a few hours I was worried you weren't well and... I'm sorry.'

'You don't have to be sorry, but I'm OK, I'm not unwell today. I feel... happy. For the first time in a long while.'

'You do, really?' The elation filling his voice touches her heart.

'I do.'

'Nik, that's...' he always goes quiet when he's trying not to cry.

'It's alright.' She makes the turn into her bedroom. A room that looks brighter than normal. It was once a symbol of failure, the bed a place of retreat. She sits in front of her rarely-used dresser. 'I didn't mean to worry you, I'm sorry. I'll keep my phone with me in future. I can't wait until you come home. I miss you.'

'I miss you too.' He tries not to sniffle. He's waited so long to hear that she feels OK. She couldn't have given him a better gift to kiss away his fears and anxieties. She opens a deep drawer at the bottom of her jewellery box.

'Al... thank you.'

'What for?'

'For the prism, and for what you see in me. For loving me. For everything you do for me. You make such a difference, and I don't tell you that enough. I love you so much.'

'Nik I...' He takes a shaky breath on the other end of the line. 'I love you too. More than anyone. You mean everything to me, I just wanted you to see that, I felt you had to know. I thought it might help.'

'It did. It's helped me realise so much about myself. So much I couldn't see, or wasn't willing to.' She does sound different, even to herself. Confident. Clear and strong.

'Where's the prism now?' She places it carefully into the drawer and touches it once more before closing it.

'It's in a safe place. I understand what it… what you were trying to tell me. It'll always be with me whether I'm holding it or not.' She moves to the wardrobes and opens the door with the full length mirror on the other side. Nik takes in her reflection, looking at the face staring back at her, truly seeing it for the first time... and grins with joy and acceptance.

# EPILOGUE

As Alastair steps out of the taxi and stands at the end of his own driveway a week earlier than he expected to be home, he knows he's made the right decision. The air smells fresh and familiar. His stomach flips with anticipation of seeing the reaction on Nik's face when he enters the house. He never did tell her he'd be back early and he so rarely gets chance to surprise her.

Paying the driver he fails to keep a wide grin from decorating his face. Goosebumps rise on his arms at the thought of getting to wrap them around Nik at long last. What will he find when he sees her? From the phone alone he can tell something has begun to change in her.

He's not naïve enough to think she'll never have a bad day again. Depression doesn't lose its grip so easily, but knowing he has helped provide the tools she can use to fight it more effectively brings a beaming sense of joy.

Each step closer to the house he hopes she doesn't see him by chance through a window. The rolling suitcase wheels would give him away, and so he carries it to the doorstep, trying not to shuffle his luggage around too much. Part of his mind dreads finding the house quiet and the bedroom dark, back to square one, but he pushes the possibility aside.

He opens the door as quietly as he can, but then worries that he might scare her if he's too quiet. Especially as she's been living alone for almost three months, frightening her is the last thing he wants. The closing of the door echoes through the house and he takes a deep breath. The smell of home is always a little different after being away for a while.

'Nik?' No answer. Was she out? He leaves the luggage in the hall and makes his way through to the kitchen. The house is spotlessly clean for the most part, but he can follow a trail of Nik's actions from the few items he can see.

A plate of toast crumbs by the sink, a coffee mug in the living room on the side-table and a blanket balled up on the sofa. A dressing gown hangs over the banister as he makes his way upstairs. A faint, fast tapping sound trickles out through the open office door.

She's pulling the same face she always does when she's focusing. Brow slightly creased, eyes tracking the letters as they appear on her screen, and large high-quality headphones relaying audio to her ears.

He leans against the door, smiling just at the sight of her. She's dressed, hair brushed, and even from this distance it looks as though she's dropped a tiny bit of weight, not that he ever thought she needed to. She's holding herself differently, sitting straighter and missing the usual musk of guilt or tiredness that used to plague her. It's nostalgic in a way. He hasn't seen her like this for a long time.

She still hasn't noticed him, and he almost feels bad knowing that he'll inevitably scare her by getting her attention, but he refuses to wait any longer to hold her. He knocks on the office door and she startles, whipping her head around with wide eyes. She slowly pulls the headphones off of her ears and puts them on the desk, her face turns from fear into a huge smile that matches his own.

'You're back?'

'Sorry to scare you, I shouted when I came in but I guess you didn't hear. You were so serious and focused.' Nik blushes, fights back happy tears and leaps from her chair into his waiting arms. Happiness mingled with a sense of pride washes over him as her arms wrap around his waist and she buries her cheek into his chest. The familiar vanilla of her body wash and coconutty hint of her shampoo is the real smell of home. 'I missed you so much.'

'How come you're back early? Not that I'm complaining.'

'I wanted to surprise you, with the coming home bit at least. As for the company, I backed out of the acquisition.'

'You did, why?'

'I'll tell you about it later, first things first. You look amazing.' He expects the uncomfortable flinch that usually follows a compliment, but instead he's greeted with a humble dropping of the eyes and a gentle response.

'Th-thank you. I dusted off the exercise bike.'

'I don't mean your weight, though I can tell you've lost a little. Even though you never needed to. I mean you in general. You look great. Healthy, happy, and as lovely as ever.'

'I've had one or two days where I've done nothing but sit around, but I'm trying my best.'

'It's working, whatever you're doing. Maybe I should go away more often,' he jibes.

'No, I'd rather you didn't.' She hugs him again, still beaming, and rises on her tip-toes to kiss him. It's been a long while since she's done that, too. This is the woman he fell in love with. The woman he will always love.

'I could do with a cup of British coffee. It's not quite the same over there.'

'I'll make it, just let me save my work.' She bounces over to the computer, clicking here and there and putting the headphones back on charge. Then she grabs his hand and starts to lead him downstairs. 'You're going to have to fill me in on why you backed out of the merger. Maybe if the weather is still nice later we can go for a walk together too, I found a nice little walking trail behind the house that I didn't even know was there.'

She's not completely different, but the change in her is stark yet subtle at the same time. Her mannerisms the same but altered, her way of speaking similar but not. An old and a new Nik combined. All positive changes, all giving hope for the future.

He'll still be there for the inevitable bad days, but today he fights back happy tears and brims with love for the beautiful, strong woman leading him to the kitchen.

END

# ACKNOWLEDGEMENTS

Prism is a very personal story for me. The most personal of all the stories I've published so far. Many of the problems that Nik carries are ones that I used to struggle with myself, so writing this story was very cathartic.

I wanted to share it to let others who struggle with similar things know that you aren't alone in how you feel. And that no matter what your own version of Nothing inside your head tells you, you are enough and always will be. You can overcome this.

I want to add a special thank you to Fran, fellow writer and fabulous friend, for this project. Ever since you read this story as a beta reader, years ago, you seem to have kept it alive in your heart and thoughts. That means the world to me, and gives me hope that it might be that way for other readers too. I can only aspire to return the same level of fantastic support you've endlessly offered over the past 5 years. I'll always be cheering for you!

The idea for this story came from my wonderful partner, James, who made me wish I could see myself the way he seems to because it was so far removed from the way I saw myself. Both inside and out. So thank you James, for helping me to see that I don't need to understand why or how you see me the way you do, I just have to be willing to accept it.

You helped me realise that the negative voice inside my head wasn't the truth, just another opinion. And that opinions aren't immutable truths or facts. They can be questioned, disagreed with, or denied entirely.

Your compassion and patience, support and love over the years have helped me overcome so much. I wouldn't be who I am now without the safe space you provided for me to grow, learn, and come to love who I am. I know I'll have blips in the future. Some big, some small, but your strength helps me be stronger too.

My amazing readers, this story is not a cure-all but hopefully it's a start. Keep being your wonderful selves, and thank you for giving this story a chance!

Printed in Great Britain
by Amazon